GIBSON'S MELODY

Last Score Novella

K.L. SHANDWICK

Gibson's Melody
A Last Score Novella
K.L. SHANDWICK
©2017

ACKNOWLEDGMENTS

Editor: Andie.M. Long Editing and Proofreading service
Cover Design: by Francessca Wingfield
Cover Images: Anuki @ A.Chumburidze Photography and K.L. Shandwick
Cover Model: Joseph Wareham
Beta Readers: Elmarie Pieterse, Sarah Lintott, Donna Trippi Salzano
Proof readers Lisa Perkins, Sue Noyes, and Kim Gray.

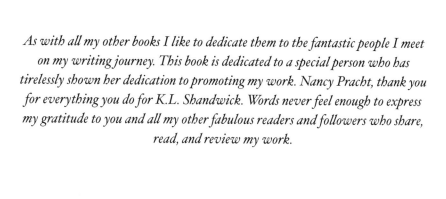

As with all my other books I like to dedicate them to the fantastic people I meet on my writing journey. This book is dedicated to a special person who has tirelessly shown her dedication to promoting my work. Nancy Pracht, thank you for everything you do for K.L. Shandwick. Words never feel enough to express my gratitude to you and all my other fabulous readers and followers who share, read, and review my work.

PROLOGUE

Piper

RELENTLESS FAT TEARS FLOWED STEADILY DOWN MY FACE, STAINING my pale grief-stricken cheeks. No seventeen year old girl should be in my position. No girl on the cusp of womanhood should have to say goodbye to the one woman who is bonded to her like no other. For most of the funeral I felt detached from reality until I stood by the graveside.

Snapping back to reality, I dragged my eyes away from the fancy oak coffin with the too expensive handles, and saw the solemn but sympathetic face of the elderly priest. He gave me a slow nod of encouragement and prompted me to carry out my final duty.

A large strong hand gently squeezed my shoulder. I glanced up at his face through blurry tearful eyes and met the compassionate stare of the man I owed my future to. Stepping forward my breath hitched and a strangled sob tore from my throat as another wave of overwhelming emotion hit me. *This is it.* For over a week I'd feared this very second in time but when it came, I had just wanted it to be over.

Inhaling a deep shuddery breath I crouched low to the ground and grabbed a small handful of powdery dirt from the mound of earth piled at the edge of the grave. My fingernails scratched at the arid soil as they scraped through it. Closing my fingers, I stood up straight with a fistful in the palm of my hand. Just then he was right where I needed him to be, wrapping a supportive muscular arm tentatively around my waist.

Courage crept up from deep within me until it flowed steadily at his caring touch. He was the most unlikely hero, but he was definitely mine. Like some kind of guardian angel, he had swept in and caught me at a time when I was helpless and felt in freefall. "You can do this, baby. Take a deep breath and do what you gotta," he said, in his gentle deep Southern drawl as he kissed my temple and held me reassuringly against his strong, warm body.

My eyes closed momentarily as I tried to shut out my horror of losing her forever. *This is the moment when I sever the ties that bound me to the woman who's been there through all of my suffering, just as I had been there through most of hers. She didn't deserve any of this and I hate God for taking her from me after everything we've suffered. I love you, Mom. I'll never forget you.* I stepped closer to the edge of the grave.

The noise of the dirt scattering over her casket as it lay in the deep hole sounded hollow— final. I couldn't bear to look down at it in the ground and turned into the warm protective arms of the man standing beside me. I was thankful for the deliberately tight hug he gave me.

"Good girl, I got you. Your mama would have been proud of you, sweetheart," he said, soothingly while his hand gently rubbed my back. "Come on, let's get you out of here before someone recognizes me and it turns into a circus," he encouraged gently in his soft tone.

I let him guide me to the safety of the luxurious black limousine, transport I could not have afforded, had it not been for him. I felt dazed. A vein in my head pulsed with a throbbing headache I'd had for several days from all the crying I'd done.

Johnny, the driver, opened the door and I slid in beside Chloe, who was already seated. "Come here, sweetheart," she coaxed with a sympathetic smile and wrapped her arms around me in another tight hug.

A new wave of grief washed over me and I fell apart with relief that the duty I'd dreaded was finally over. Sobbing into her shoulder I felt no shame at sharing my grief. "Let it out, honey. It's okay, we're here for you," she said in a kind and gentle tone.

Somehow it felt easier to cry in the arms of people who knew what it was like to live the kind of life I'd led, and I felt Chloe definitely knew. They both did. That's how Mom and I met them. Mom trusted them when she had trusted no one in years. She said the couple supporting me had saved us. From how my mom's violent and abusive partner had been treating us for the longest time I knew she was probably right.

Living in a world where your abuser also served your needs was a pretty delicate path to tread. We accepted all he gave us because my mom felt we had no other choice. The slaps, the bruises, insults, and the fear he instilled, because we knew no other way and for a long time it appeared as if there was no escape.

Mostly we stayed because my mom was broken; a shell of the person she was because he changed her and made her believe she wasn't worthy of anything else.

However, our abuser was also the breadwinner. He fed and clothed us, kept a roof over our heads and so we accepted his terrifying behaviour and managed the best we could. At least that was how my mom saw our situation.

My beautiful gentle mom and I had been through hell for as long as I could remember. She was resigned to the life my father dealt us, but tried her best to protect me from his cruel and harsh behaviour. She taught me some survival skills and to be resourceful at finding ways of staying out of our home until around an hour before bedtime.

If only she'd taken her own advice. There was no such escape from him for her...the man she'd lived with half of her life. Every day since I'd been born she'd lived her life in terror and always tried to meet his demands to keep him happy.

The man was insistent that I called him Dad, wasn't my dad at all. Colin had gotten with my mom when she was pregnant with me. Frightened and vulnerable, she was a nineteen year old girl, who'd made a mistake by having her one and only one night stand and he was older, in his thirties.

Thinking the guy would be someone who'd take care of her she'd settled for him. I remember her saying that being in love hadn't mattered to her, being looked after when she had me to provide for was more important. In reality, the way he'd treated her she'd have been better off as a single mom.

Working as a backing singer for a semi-famous act when she met him they had toured the club circuits in the state of Ohio together. Apparently he had a silver tongue and an easy going nature back in the day. She'd felt at the time he was "Protective and cool," but after she'd had me and regained her figure, his personality started to change.

When she started singing with the band again Colin's jealousy and insecurity got the better of him. According to her he got into regular fist-fights with guys he figured were after her. Mom said it was all in his head but from that point on the manipulation and brain washing had begun until she was out on a limb, cut off from all her friends, and a battered, stay-at-home mom to me.

We relished in the times when he worked away. Those were our golden times because we relaxed our guards. The atmosphere in our home felt instantly light and unoppressive. It was like we breathed deeply when he was gone.

During those precious days it was like my mom would suddenly come to life and a whole different person would climb out. Watching her eyes fill with emotion instead of the dead expression that was there when he was present, was everything. Her smile lit up the room and her laugh was infectious. Whenever I saw her like that I wished it could be that way all the time.

Usually, I had to wait a couple of hours after he'd gone to see that side of her, because she had to convince herself he wasn't going to come back unexpectedly. Once she was sure it was safe we'd head to Colin's closet, drag out his vinyl long-playing record collection, and listen to the coolest bands from the 70s 80s and 90s.

Listening to her talk about music gave me a glimpse into the world she'd lived in before she'd met Colin. The passion and understanding of the emotional lyrics made me enthralled to hear her talk about them.

Maybe—she was extremely talented as a singer as well as being knowledgeable. Her voice touched me so much I cried when she sang. Secretly she passed her skills onto me, and taught me so much, like how to breathe properly, to control my voice, blending and scaling octaves from my chest voice to my head voice smoothly. We worked on strengthening my diaphragm and voice projection until my range was extensive and I could sing practically anything.

Of course our time was limited and it was done without Colin being aware because he had forbidden my mom from listening to music unless he was there to call the shots. He never allowed my mom to sing...ever and if she hummed along he'd switch the turntable off and put the records away. It was torturous to watch how quickly he'd flip from the sublime to ridiculous in his behavior just because he knew music made her happy and that wasn't part of his plan for her.

My love of singing also made me happy and as Colin was brought up in a religious family he let me join the church choir. What he didn't know was that allowed me to practice honing my voice and gave me confidence to sing in front of an audience. It also helped me temporarily escape the crappy life I led at home.

Mom said music was in my blood and I'd always wanted to play the piano, but Colin flat out said it would be a waste of money. *"No one earned a living playing piano unless you were Stevie Wonder or a classical prodigy,"* he remarked. That was rich coming from the guy who earned his living working for musicians. His comment only made me more determined to prove him wrong.

Without proper music lessons my voice became my instrument. Colin couldn't take that away from me. He was careful what he said and did about that because the school included me in the music recitals and from the moment I hit high school I was selected for all the main singing roles in school plays and performances. The constant praise from my teachers and my mom gave me all the encouragement I needed to keep going.

Although I was popular, I wasn't liked by some of the cliques who felt they should have been given the character parts allocated to me, purely because they were richer and felt entitled. They were no barrier after dealing with someone like Colin and their attitudes only made me more determined. Like my mom said, money can't buy brains or talent. I wasn't a glory hound, but I fought for those roles as I believed if I was good enough it just may have been the one thing that could have led to a better life for me and my mother.

Burying the single most precious person I loved with all my heart was by far the toughest thing I'd ever faced and I imagined it to be the hardest thing I'd ever do in my lifetime. Everything we'd worked so hard to achieve in the previous nine months had happened too late. All our efforts appeared pointless since she died.

Trying to be optimistic wasn't something I could stomach at the time but Chloe was more optimistic than me and worked on the philosophy life's turns happened for a reason. Who knew maybe she was right, because Mom never knew she was sick when I saw the flyer for Dignity Safe House and rang the Freephone number. Had she known I'd have probably been standing at a pauper's grave with my mother's partner.

The stars must have aligned that day, because Colin had left for Denver City that morning and within three hours of calling Chloe's charity, we were sitting in a blacked-out SUV with all we could carry, crossing the state line. It was a sixteen hour drive to Colorado and when the driver informed us we only had one more hour to go the transformation in my mom's face was incredible.

I'd never been to the mountains before. It felt like it took forever to get there but with every mile after that stretched behind us I could see life being breathed back into my mom. She was petrified as was I, but something about the woman's calm and soothing voice on the call I made gave me the confidence I need to believe she'd keep us safe.

When I first brought up the subject of escaping Colin's clutches my mom was terrified but when I threatened to go without her it was all the persuasion she'd needed to make the jump. There was no way for her to know I'd never have left her but I didn't feel guilty. It broke my heart to let her think I'd leave her behind but I was desperate and she'd taught me that sometimes it was necessary to be cruel to be kind.

Setting up somewhere else takes time, but with the support Chloe's team offered would see us relocated in a matter of months and just when I thought, *God is good* my mom started complaining of headaches. Apparently the changes in Mom hadn't gone unnoticed by Chloe despite the short time she'd known her and the day she fainted, Chloe wasted no time in calling the retreat physician, insisting my mom see her.

When the doctor came I had no idea our journey to Colorado would mark the beginning of the end for my mom. I remember the day I learned of her fate like it was yesterday. Chloe and the retreat doctor sat down with me and gently delivered the devastating news that my mother had cancer, it was terminal and she only had a short time to live. No one could imagine the pain those words brought me.

Shocked and terrified, I screamed in disbelief that they were lying. Mom was too young to die and they were wrong. I became angry and immediately went into denial. Sadly they were telling the truth. My mom died never seeing her fortieth birthday.

She barely made it eleven weeks after we found out and instead of us preparing to move out like all the other domestic abuse survivors, we were given one of the little apartments on the other side of the main building that was normally reserved for staff.

For the last month and a half of her life I lived alone supported by the refuse staff, Chloe and her husband. My thoughts were a mess and I couldn't see past the point when my mom was no longer around. It felt selfish, but I was frightened of what would happen to me.

Chapter One
LEVELLING OUT
Piper

CHLOE BARCLAY WAS THE DIRECTOR OF THE CHARITY THAT BECAME our safe haven from the abuse we'd run from. She was stunningly beautiful with those massive soulful eyes, a gentle, soft voice, and an incredibly kind and humble person.

When Mom and I reached the ranch retreat the quiet calm of the environment was so far removed from what I'd grown up in, it felt strange and uncomfortable.

When we arrived near midnight a hot supper was ready and waiting. The staff on duty were warm, friendly, and empathetic toward us. It helped us to feel welcome. While we ate, our assigned keyworker, Elenor, came into the communal dining area to meet us and as we filled our stomachs she gave us some history about the place.

Gibson Barclay funded his wife, Chloe, who built the secluded refuge facility for battered women and hand-picked a team of experts in everything from housing, education, family therapies, and financial aid.

The small-storey blocks of two and three bedroomed apartment units housed twenty-six families at any one time. As well as emotional support, the refuge staff arranged tailor-made support relocation packages to every state of America to ensure the safety of those in their care safe from falling prey to their previous abusers.

Advice in the form of how to keep safe, welfare plans, accommodation, and help with resumes had helped many women from abusive backgrounds retrain or find jobs.

After we'd eaten, a dark-haired woman of around fifty called Margaret took us to our accommodation. She gave us some further literature to read through before she left us to settle in for the night. As soon as the door latch clicked and we were left alone we glanced around the clean, simply furnished living room of the apartment and burst into tears. They were tears of relief because we'd made it.

Almost ten hours after we went to bed I woke to find my mom sitting staring out of the window at the beautiful snow peaked mountains. I slid out of bed and wandered toward her. Her head snapped around as frightened eyes connected with mine for a second before she released her breath and sighed heavily. "Sorry, old habits die hard," she said, dryly. I slid my arm around her neck and hugged her from behind.

"Couldn't sleep?"

"Headache," she offered.

"It's okay, Mom, we made it."

She stared anxiously back at me and although I could see she was still fraught with worry, she gave me a half-smile. "Yeah, we did," she said in a relieved tone as she patted my hand.

Soft knocking on the door drew our attention toward it and I went to see who was there. A young girl stood hugging a basket of toiletries under one arm and carried some fresh towels in the other.

"Breakfast is going to be cleared away in a few minutes. It's almost 11:00 am. Chloe asked me to come and tell you, she'd like to meet with you right before lunch at 1:00 pm. Her office is on the first floor, second door on the left."

I smiled as she slid the basket from her hand to mine and without waiting for me to reply, she headed back down the corridor. I was ravenous and knew my mom wouldn't even have thought about eating so I prompted her to get dressed.

Mom went through the motions of dressing still preoccupied by her change in circumstances. I knew if I didn't push her she'd forget to eat. We were opposites in that trait— anxiety made me hungry.

I wasn't used to people pulling together and doing their best to help each other, but I quickly got the sense of a community that worked together. What was different about the refuge from others I'd read about was there were men present. Chloe's view was domestic violence didn't just happen to women. Anyone who had a genuine need was never turned away if there was space.

Coming from a hostile environment I was freaked in the beginning when people openly hugged each other. Once it was explained it was part of the therapeutic techniques to break the barriers of the negative contact the families had at home it made sense. The newer ones flinched, a wary look on their faces while those that had been there for a while instigated those hugs.

The only time I ever saw everyone on the same page was if Chloe or Gibson hugged them. Every man, woman, and child in that community accepted their goodness and kind words simply because they had provided sanctuary.

———

For the rest of that day I remember how Mom looked nervously around her and I knew she had started to fear for her future, even though I thought at the time nothing could have been worse than she'd already been through. Little did I know breaking free from Colin was the least of my worries.

I would never have connected the name Chloe Barclay at Safe Houses with Gibson Barclay, the larger-than-life rock God. When she gave me her name I figured it was coincidental, but when I saw her I instantly knew it was Gibson's wife.

There had never been any pretentious behavior from Chloe. She was one of the most humbled people I'd ever met. Mom said she was my guardian angel after Chloe had welcomed us into the safety of her safe house. From day one we were treated equally at the refuge but that quickly changed when our situation changed after just one week when Mom fell sick. Mom had complained of headaches and was found collapsed on the floor in the corridor.

Memories of that hellish time were cloudy, like everything happened in a blur. Initially, staff thought it due to the changes in her emotional state because it was common for women to arrive at the refuge malnourished, and usually physically and emotionally fragile after being removed from the stress of their abuse.

When Mom was no better that evening Chloe asked for more tests to be done. Four hours later Mom had a full body scan which revealed the devastating news. Yet further investigations uncovered a very aggressive form of breast cancer with metastases of the brain. I was stunned. Mom had never complained of anything apart from headaches and occasional twinges in her back.

Being told her cancer was extensive and the only treatment open to her was palliative care made me freak out. I thought my heart would break after all we'd been through and for that to happen to her.

Watching my mom cry and apologize for being sick was heart breaking. She was more scared about leaving me behind than dying. I felt selfish for being petrified about my future alone and even considered taking my own life to be with her.

Seeing my mother fade day after day was the scariest and loneliest time in my life. Instead of starting a new life together where we got to experience a life without fear, hers was rapidly ending.

After a fortnight Mom's decline was visible from hour to hour. One day I'd try to be brave the next I'd break down and crumple at the foot of her bed with grief. Chloe and her team were supportive and +tried to be reassuring but at seventeen years old how could anyone reassure me I'd be okay when my only parent was going to die?

Whenever I was around her I tried to stay calm but as soon as I left her bedside I became vicious and angry, lashing out whenever one of the staff tried to placate me. Even on the days I felt I couldn't face being with her Chloe encouraged me to spend every waking moment with my Mom.

When Gibson arrived home from a short tour away I was surprised when he and Chloe came to see me together. I hadn't seen him around since the day after we'd arrived and took it to be his visits were more about seeing Chloe than anything to do with the center. But that didn't fit either because I saw how everyone else embraced him with a comfortable familiarity and figured we'd just arrived as he'd left.

Gibson and Chloe had obviously discussed me and had thought ahead to the time when my mom was no longer around. Very tactfully and with great sensitivity they dealt with the elephant in the room. I was still a minor and when my mom passed I'd be an orphan.

With Mom's agreement legal papers were hastily drawn up by Gibson's lawyers and after discussing my status with my mom, he and Chloe became my legal guardians. I asked how long that would be for and his initial response was a sincere sad smile and a piercing look.

He reached for my hand and pulled me into a hug and made me feel safe immediately. "For as long as you want us, darlin'," he'd said. I leaned back and stared at him in disbelief because my whole experience from the moment I'd arrived at the ranch had been life-changing, but not in the way I'd expected.

The situation I had found myself in was bizarre. It felt like some psychedelic dream I'd wake up from, but it wasn't. I stood was wrapped in the arms of Rock God, Gibson Barclay, and I had just listened to him as he conducted an incredibly detailed conversation with my Mom about my future and agreed to parent me.

Facing up to some of the thoughts that I'd buried in the back of my mind still felt horrendous, but his words touched me in a way I could never explain. Tears burned in my throat as my heart both relaxed and squeezed.

A rock star and his wife had agreed to keep me safe, and for most teenagers that would have been sick. For me it only made the reality of my mom's death more vivid in my mind. The best I could feel was they had made the most devastating time in my life a little easier to face.

———

My future without family felt overwhelming. For the first week after the burial I had lived in a defeated daze. I was furious with God, myself, and I hoped I never showed it, but with my mom for leaving me alone.

Angry thoughts constantly swam inside my head and festered in my belly because she couldn't find it in her to fight anymore. And I felt even worse whenever I thought about how we'd finally started to live the lives we were supposed to have only to find out my mom had already begun dying. She was so sick that by the time she was diagnosed with her cancer it was too late. In my darkest moments, I had wanted to die too.

Eleven days after the funeral Chloe knocked on my studio door. She'd been really kind but when she stated that she knew how it felt to have no-one at a vulnerable time I almost bit her head off. I stared in anger and felt patronized. I thought she had no idea how I really felt and thought she said it to comfort me. Just as I was about to blow I saw a pained look pass through her eyes and knew instantly she really did understand my needs.

We talked openly into the night and I was surprised by her confident parental approach to helping me figure out what I'd do next. I was determined to graduate. I owed that to my mom. She'd suffered everything Colin had dished out in the hope I'd have a better life than she had.

When I had left school so abruptly my non-attendance elsewhere had put me behind with my studies, but I was still afraid and I didn't want to attend another school in case Colin tracked me down. He was devious, and clever, and I knew he'd find some way of getting to me. The thought of ever seeing him again gave me made me sick after what he put my beautiful mom through.

Even though Gibson and Chloe said they'd be my guardians I still felt weird because I'd already extended my stay at their retreat. When I voiced this to Chloe she agreed.

"You're right. We didn't want to push you and seem insensitive to your grief but the longer you are here the less help we can offer to another family in need."

My heart sank and I knew we had nothing. Gibson had already settled all the legal and medical bills associated with my family and I thought it wasn't appropriate for me to continue school when I had to pay my way.

Facing up to the future was the last thing on my mind. "I'm sorry,

Chloe. If I can just stay until I find work or I can sleep in the barn or something."

Chloe's eyes widened in shock. "Jeez, Piper. No. I meant you should move into the house. Gibson and I are going to take care of you for however long you want. Lifelong if you want us. Trust me, we're not just carrying out a paper exercise with you, honey. I'll speak to the housekeeper about your room. Maybe you'd like to come over and pick out which one you'd feel most comfortable in?"

Choked with emotion I swallowed three times past the lump in my throat as my eyes welled with tears. "Come here, honey, I know it's a huge ask at a time when you're feeling so vulnerable but believe me, Gibson and I will do everything we can to help you become part of our family."

Stepping into her arms I let the tears flow because I no longer had the strength to hide how I felt as I allowed relief to wash over me. Whenever Gibson and Chloe held me it had felt like the home I'd never had. Gibson like the protector I'd never experienced and Chloe like the one person in the world who got where my head was at. I was still extremely grief-stricken but mingled amongst moments where I was able to breath. At those times I told myself there was hope.

Chapter Two

SOBERING MOMENT

Gibson

"WHO WANTS TO PARTY WITH US?" I YELLED AND POINTED AT THE weedy looking nerdy guy with the long straggly hair and square rimmed spectacles in the front row. Droplets of sweat dripped from my hair and stung my eyes, as the heat beat down relentlessly from the spotlights suspended above me. I lifted the hem of my sodden T-shirt and wiped my face.

The crowd went berserk when I gave them a glimpse of my body and all I was doing was trying to see. Glancing further along, I saw five college girls all in a row, one sweet looking with her perfectly straight black hair. They were just a few of the thousands of girls sat with their tongues hanging out wanting a piece of me.

At one time I'd have nodded at one and they'd have been hanging back waiting for me after the gig, but my life was so far removed from the manwhore I was then, to where I am now. My mind flashed back to the sweltering conditions we'd been used to in the cramped bars we performed in night after night. Those girls were essential to my performance both during and after the gigs. They sure kept me trim...fucking and running. The lifestyle of a teenage musician was pretty awesome if a bit chaotic but playing music and getting laid was what I used to live for.

Glancing down at the audience the sweet angelic face of a girl smiled widely up at me. It tugged at my heartstrings but not in the way you'd think. Chloe and I had been trying for a kid of our own and by that night we were down to hoping for a miracle.

Some would say it was a good thing I hadn't been blessed with a kid, but they'd have been judging Gibson the boy. Gibson the man was determined to be a bigger man, and that was all down to the love of a good woman—Chloe.

Had my mom been alive she'd have told me you get what you're given in this world and not what you want. If that was true then the good Lord had decided that kids weren't to figure in our future. Without going into it too much when I found out what the problem was I was glad that Kace, Chloe's ex-partner, was still serving his twenty year sentence for what he did to her.

In the beginning Chloe couldn't see past my manwhore legacy and for a while there I guess I couldn't see past hers. Kace's promiscuity had left Chloe infertile which was a bum deal considering she'd only ever been with two guys. The news left Chloe devastated and when she found out she had wanted to leave me. Even although she was hurting badly she had still been thoughtful enough not to want to deny me the chance to have a child because of a bad choice she'd made.

Convincing her that what happened, or the consequences of that were her fault wasn't easy but eventually I wore her down. It took a lot of love and persistence and gradually she accepted I'd rather have her than ten kids in my life. To me it wasn't the end of the world because I figured we could still spread our love by caring for others.

My eyes scanned the crowds again and a small dark haired girl with huge brown eyes caught my gaze. We connected in that second a flash-back image almost threw me off my lyrics. Heavy eye make-up couldn't disguise my familiarity to her. My eyes roamed over her then I noticed a kid beside her holding a placard up which said, 'Gibson and Kiran 2008'. I glanced at the kid's T-shirt. In bright silver glittery letters, emblazoned across the front it read, 'Made in Chicago'. My heart literally stopped for a beat.

Kiran? The name was unusual but I'd heard it before. Closing my eyes for a second I tried to draw an image from the recesses of my mind but nothing emerged.

Turning to Mick I wandered over and shouted in his ear, "Ten o'clock about eight rows back. You get the same vibe from that message as I'm getting," I asked. Mick continued to play but moved across to their side of the stage for a better look. "Damn, looks like a lawsuit in the making," he shouted back when he came back over to me.

"Shit." My world fell from under my feet and turned toward Syd, my manager who stood in the wings. Nodding at Mick he knew instinctively what I wanted as I exited the stage to have a word with him.

"What the fuck's wrong?" He asked bending forward with his hand cupped over his ear.

"There's a woman with a kid out there and I think she's mine."

"You're fucking joking, right?"

"I wish—" I stood feeling helpless.

"And I wish I had a Buck for every woman that's claimed you're the father of their baby," he chuckled, brushing it off because we'd faced accusations before.

"Not this one. I got a feeling. Shit," I replied and ran my hand through my sweat-soaked hair. I felt blindsided by the image of the girl still in my head while Mick did his best to cover for my absence on stage. Len continued to play a repetitive cyclic percussion on the drums but glared in a what-the-fuck-get-your-ass-back-out-here look.

"Why do you think there's something in this?"

"I've got a photograph of my mom as a kid and this one looks the spitting image of her."

"You sure? I mean it's dark n'all." The grim look he gave me said what I already knew. I'd be swimming in shit with Chloe if what I felt in my gut was true.

"Invite them backstage. I can't think—" I fell silent leaving him standing there as I made my way back out on stage to the roar of the crowd. I made a joke about drinking too much and having to take a leak in the middle of the concert. The audience laughed in unison and I launched straight into the next song.

For most of the following song my eyes were glued to the woman and the child. It was fortunate it wasn't one of the newer songs I was singing at the time so I did that on autopilot while my mind continually sifted through my vague memories. There were only a few I remembered during the year before I met up with Chloe again and then it came to me. The girl with the kid was a stripper I'd fucked one night when I was wasted.

Jesus, Chloe is gonna have my balls.

Chloe and I had been together for almost seven years and the kid looked like she was in the right age range to have been conceived before I met her—but not by much. Instinctively I knew the kid was mine.

What an almighty clusterfuck. Just when I'd secured Piper's position. My heart wasn't in the rest of the gig. It was too busy lying at the bottom of my stomach and I couldn't wait for the show to be done. Instead of three encore songs we played two then I called it a night. Drenched in sweat my chest felt tight with anxiety.

Before Chloe I lived how I wanted to and never answered to anyone. I never made excuses for who I was and I never gave a damn who I screwed. The only criteria I had for women was they consented, were pretty and available. The rest either happened or it didn't.

Over the years my management had acted swiftly to quash claim after claim I had from women who wanted their kid named as mine, and until my eyes settled on the raven haired kid with the big brown eyes not one had proven true. But this time...I didn't need a DNA test, even from thirty feet away I was able to spot my kin instantly.

Mick slapped my back and grabbed my attention. "What the fuck is the deal?" he asked with a concerned look in his eyes.

"Did you see her, Dude? Syd's having them brought backstage,"

Lennox jogged and caught up with me as I walked purposefully down the long narrow corridor back to the dressing room.

"What the hell was going on with you out there? You looked like you'd seen a ghost."

"Excellent choice of words, Len. I may well have." Len studied my poker face.

"You care to fill me in, Gib? I have no fucking clue what was going on out there."

"Someone in the audience spooked him. She had a kid with her and the placard alluded to the possibility she's his." Mick replied before I could answer.

"And you're takin' this one seriously?"

Staring intensely at me, I saw the way his head coiled back in reaction to my expression I knew he had his answer.

Most of the time, Chloe tried to tag along to the gigs but if it was more than five days at a time she flew back to the refuge retreat service she'd built from scratch to keep on top of things. God must have been looking down on me because the gig we were playing was a one time gig and I was flying back tomorrow. Chloe had decided to stay home to support our new charge, Piper, who was still grieving the death of her mom.

Piper was a great kid with a good head on her shoulders but lacked stability of any family around her. She reminded me of myself at that age and I wanted nothing more than to help Chloe support her. After discussing with her mom we'd sought legal guardianship and promised her we'd keep her daughter safe for as long as Piper wanted that. Personally, after seeing how Chloe took on the role I wished she'd stay with us forever.

A knock on the door brought me out of my daydream. "Yeah," I asked pulling my wet T-shirt over my head. Syd shoved the door open and caught my attention immediately. "I've asked Simon to use his room and moved him in with Mick for now. You wanna get changed and meet them in there. I thought discretion was the best course of action in these circumstances, we don't want the press to get wind before Chloe if she does turn out to be yours," he said informing me of the arrangements.

"Do you think she looks like me?"

"Nope, but if you say she's like your mom, did she resemble you?"

"Nah, she was gorgeous, look at me...wait, fuck it that won't work 'cause I'm a good-looking man as well," I joked. My smile dropped because Syd could see my nerves through my bravado.

"To be honest Syd, the way I threw my dick around I'm

surprized there aren't more kids out there. When we were having fertility tests I was sure it was me who was firing blanks or thought my swimmers that were left were exhausted from all the coming I'd done. Finding out it was Chloe who had the issues came as one helluva shock."

Syd smirked at reasoning but nodded in agreement, "She's gonna be heartbroken, Gibson." His comment ripped a hole in my chest.

"Yeah she is and I'll feel like the biggest shit on the planet for making her feel that way. You know me. Chloe's happiness has always been my priority since the first day I got with her." Staring me out I could see Syd had no words of comfort for me and the silence between us made the air thicken.

"Alright, get the fuck out so as I can shower and change. Let's not prolong the agony any longer than is necessary. Tell them I'll be with them in ten."

Dropping his head to look at his feet Syd began to walk toward the door before he turned. "Are you sure you want to do this, Gib? You know I can always—"

"Always what? Deny what may be my only offspring? Nah, Syd. What the fuck do you take me for? I'd never do that. I've always taken responsibility for how I behaved despite the way I lived my life. I'm not ashamed of who I am or who I did, but I won't turn my back on any kid that's mine. That's not a man who does that." Syd stood quietly considering what I'd said.

"The only person I'd ever apologize to for the way I lived before is my wife. I lived to the max and no matter how it affected those around me, I'll accept my fate with this one. Chloe is my number one priority in life and Piper became number two from the moment I signed those papers, if this little girl turns out to belong to me then I'm fucked if I won't take care of her."

"I'm proud to know you, Gibson. There's not many who'd feel the way you do faced with something like this...there's many who'd do whatever they could to keep this quiet."

"If what I think is true I'd never belittle the woman who carried my child. That's shameful for any kid to go through and I'd never wish it on anyone never mind an innocent. If that little kid has been an accidental happening it doesn't give me the right to make her suffer by rejecting her existence."

As soon as he left I stepped under the shower. The jets a welcome relief on my hot and sweaty skin. Grabbing the shower gel I filled my palm with the thick liquid and ran it over my body. A quick wash later I swiped a huge bath towel from the rack and wrapped it loosely around my waist. My heart was pounding from the mixed emotions passing through it, everything from joy to anxiety wondering if she was mine and how I'd soften the blow for Chloe.

My mind flitted between the small face I'd seen in the crowd and my beautiful wife. A loyalty to Chloe in the first form but a split forming there for a small girl I'd seen who could or would not be mine. It was a bigger mind fuck than any drugs I could have ingested. For the first time in months I wanted alcohol. That's when I knew I was stressed.

Within minutes I had pulled on a white T-shirt that stretched over my pecs and pulled it down over the dark jeans I'd stepped into. Heading for the door I didn't get time to open it before Len pushed it toward me.

"There you are. Damn, Gib I see what you mean. That picture of your mother Chloe has perched on the mantel is identical. I saw the kid when Syd's guy directed her in there," he said gesturing toward Simon's dressing room door, "that little girl could be her clone."

I swallowed past the lump in my throat wondering if I had the balls to handle the following few minutes with sensitivity but then I remembered I'd had plenty of practice dealing with kids from my charity work.

Figuring I'd draw on that to see me through I took a deep breath and realized since the moment I'd walked off the stage after the last song I'd been stalling because facing the truth of the situation would change my life in a way I'd given up on. Being a natural father. As soon as I pushed the door open my eyes connected with hers and I knew instantly the child in front of me was my daughter.

Chapter Three

HUNCH

Chloe

GLANCING AT THE THICK LOW CLOUDS IN THE SKY MADE ME FEEL anxious. Gibson was airborne and on his way back from Chicago to Breckenridge, Colorado and the weather was closing in. Gibson had thought ahead when we were building the retreat and we were fortunate to have our own runway on the far side of the hill. It was only a five-minute drive down our private road to home once he landed.

It wasn't the flight that bothered me. For some reason I'd been filled with anxiety since the previous night. When Jonny his personal protection guy and close friend called to tell me the time they'd land I figured Gibson was busy, but when he didn't call me himself like he usually did I decided to call him before they set off.

Nothing except a dire emergency kept him from making that normal call like he always did when he'd stayed away so the fact he'd got Jonny to call set alarm bells ringing immediately. Hearing the tone in his voice and the curt way he'd spoken to me during that three minute call gave me the indication I wasn't wrong.

Call it instinct but we were so attuned I always knew whenever there was trouble brewing in our lives so when I asked him straight out if there was a problem, he'd deflected the question with one of his own. A minute later he concluded the call because he said being on his cell was preventing them from taking off.

All afternoon my mind wandered back to how Gibson had changed the subject and it gnawed at me until I felt an ache in my stomach and by nightfall my eyes were trained for the jet lights breaking through the sky as he headed for home. Waiting like that was like waiting for a pan of water to boil so I stood up and turned my back on the window to encourage him to land quicker.

We were so lucky with our cabin in the mountains. It was only two miles from the retreat but on the same three thousand acreage we owned. I headed downstairs from my bedroom and found Piper sitting in front of the fire in the great room. Her knees tucked beneath her skirt and pulled up to her chest. She looked so vulnerable and the sight of her tugged at my heartstrings.

"Everything okay, honey?"

Slowly her head turned and even in the low light of the fire at dusk I recognized the devastation on her face. "Yeah...just thinking."

Moving to her quickly I dropped to my knees, "I know everything feels raw for you right now and you're completely lost but Gibson and I are here for you, Piper. When Gibson comes home we'll sit down and figure out some routines for you to help you through this terrible time. We know we can never replace your mom honey, but we'll make you feel as wanted as we can. You are wanted...sometimes things happen for a reason. Some almost break us but others make us who we become. Both Gibson and I are testament to that."

Tucking her cuff in her fingers she wiped her eyes with her sleeves. "I know. You don't know how lucky I feel that we found you guys, and at the same time I feel terrible feeling lucky after what happened to my mom. I fucking hate that Colin. If only she'd never—"

"You don't have to tell me how angry you are. Everything you're thinking about him I've had the same thoughts about someone I once knew too...but that was a lifetime ago. Trust me, Piper, don't allow yourself to become bitter and twisted about the man who doesn't deserve your time. Focus on being what your mom wanted for you instead. It will be the best feeling in the world when you stick two fingers up to the man who tried to control you."

Piper cast a sideward glance, wiped her nose with a tissue, and sniffed, "You're so wise. I can see how you became a therapy person."

"I'm not a therapist, Piper. I'm a survivor just like you are. I speak from experience and the best advice I can give you is to focus on what's positive and ignore the doubts in your head. According to your mom you could be anything you want to be in life. She believed in you that much. Prove her right. Choose what you want and go after it. Nail it and then when you have we'll find Colin and make him choke on your success."

A soft giggle left her throat temporarily lightening her mood and it was music to my ears. "Boy, remind me not to piss you off, Chloe, you sound like you got this whole retribution thing down."

I began to laugh when I heard the jet engines drawing closer and my attention was diverted. "Gibson's coming home, I'm just going to see if dinner's almost ready. You may want to go wipe that mascara streak that's running over your nose before our rock star arrives."

Piper gave me a genuine smile, "Thanks, Chloe. I mean it. I don't know where I'd be without you and Gibson."

"Don't thank us yet, Piper, you haven't lived with us," I joked and turned toward the kitchen.

————

Less than fifteen minutes later, Gibson walked through the door and the air in the house shifted with his presence. "Chloe darlin', where are you?" he called out from the hallway.

Glancing at the huge glass oven dish of lasagne in my hands I quickly placed it on the black granite worktop and made my way toward him. I didn't get very far before he stepped forward closing the space and scooped me into his chest. Giving me a crushing hug he eyed my mouth, smiled and kissed me passionately. I stifled a moan and pulled away because Piper was around.

"Damn you taste good, darlin'," he muttered in a raspy voice against my mouth as I tried to even out my breathing and heartrate. "Missed you, darlin'." The look of longing in his eyes made my legs weak.

"Missed you too, baby. Are you hungry?"

Gibson's grey eyes grew darker, his pupils dilating as lust filled his dirty mind as he let his eyes roam leisurely over my body. "Always," he answered, his eyes widening slightly as he served me a cocky smirk.

Piper came into view before I could reply so I cleared my throat, made my way back around the countertop, and tried to concentrate on the food. I squeezed my thighs together because Gibson had turned me on and his continued presence made my bones melt.

Even after all the time we'd been together there wasn't a day that went past when I hadn't stared in wonder at how amazing he looked. Dark hair, piercing grey eyes, and lips that could satisfy me for days at a time.

Oblivious as to the effect he'd had on me he began to talk to Piper, his charming, charismatic ways oozing effortlessly as he put her at her ease and drew smiles to her lips even in her grief. Distracted I took the time to study how fabulous a person Gibson was. I was so lucky because I was one of the few who saw the man behind the rock star image his public saw.

When Gibson cleared his deep voice, it startled me back to their conversation but my eyes were still trained on his beautiful face. He'd only been gone a day but I'd missed him terribly. He smirked knowingly at my mind wandering and winked before he turned and moved away, "Just gonna wash my hands darlin', food smells amazing I'll be right back," he called over his shoulder. My eyes followed his tall muscular back like one of his fans until he walked out of sight.

My man was a drop-dead-knock-out-gorgeous Rock God and although he was confident in his appearance he had no real idea of his true effect on both women and men. I believed it was perfectly within his capability to make any woman drop their panties or to turn most men gay had that been his sexual preference. Luckily for me it wasn't.

Of course, being a lead singer in a top tier band like M3rCy Gibson knew he could have any woman he wanted. Offers came in droves. I think at one time he tried to take up as many as he could, but after a time for some strange reason he set his mind on me.

For a long time I had found that impossible to believe because I was definitely plain Jane and he really was 'All That', but he came after me when I couldn't believe that possible. Ever since I'd managed to see past his legacy and focused on the man underneath I'd learned he was a generous, honest, and humble man. When I accepted that as fact I knew I could never trust anyone else to the depth that I trusted Gibson.

Making my way to the table I set the lasagne down and wandered back to the oven to grab the garlic bread. Gibson came alongside and swept my hair to the side exposing my neck. "You may wanna put that hot dish back," he murmured in my ear before trailing his tongue down my neck. Dragging it back he gripped my hair and extended my face toward him. "Kiss me," he demanded.

Conscious that Piper was at the table I pressed my lips to his and whispered, "Piper is watching."

"So I can't kiss my wife when I come home from work because my new daughter is watching me?" The way he said it I wondered if it was a joke until he turned and glanced at Piper. "You want me to pussyfoot around you or make you feel like the part of the family you now are?" he asked.

Piper smirked her face turning red and stuttered a reply, "I'd rather see a couple kissing and being affectionate any day of the week than what I experienced at home."

Gibson immediately dropped his hands from me and I watched him tense. His fists balled as he strode around the counter and stared directly at Piper. "Sweetheart, you're mine now. Anyone who comes near you will have to come through me. And trust me—that's not gonna be a fucking issue. I got you."

Instinct fired Gibson's protective side and my heart raced with his bold statement about keeping Piper safe. He'd given her mother her dying wish to keep her daughter out of harm's way when took her into our care. As soon as we laid Piper's Mom in the ground Gibson's attitude shifted from that of advisor to parent seamlessly and it had made my heart squeeze with pride when I saw how seriously he had taken his new role.

Piper's eyes filled with tears, so I called her to help me by placing the water jug and wine on the table to give her the chance to collect herself then we all sat down and Gibson began helping us dish up the food.

Minutes later we were all eating silently and it struck me we'd never had such a quiet dinner with no conversation. My gaze turned to Gibson and I could tell by the way he was eating he had something big on his mind. I mulled over whether to bring it up while Piper was at the table but then I remembered what Gibson said and figured if Piper was really going to be treated as one of us then that should start from the word go.

"Alright, out with it. Gibson Barclay, I know you. What's bugging you? Don't tell me there's nothing because I don't like liars."

"Have I ever lied to you?" he asked his eyebrow raised in question with his fork poised near his mouth.

"No, but there's always a first time," I replied.

Gibson scowled, "You know me better than that, darlin'," he replied and began poking his food on his plate with his fork.

"I do. That's why I know there's a bug up your ass. So are you gonna tell me?"

Gibson's eyes darted to Piper then back to me. Pain shot through them and the only other times I'd seen that look was when he felt helpless and something had hurt me. He glanced to Piper and I saw he wasn't ready to have this conversation.

An uneasy feeling washed over me, spurring my heart rate to spike, because from the look that passed between us it was clear whatever he was holding back was serious.

Searching his face I couldn't believe for one second he'd cheated on me. We were solid as a couple. *Weren't we?* A silent conversation happened between us right there at the table and I knew from the fleeting plea in his eyes it was something he had no control over.

Infidelity wasn't the issue. Wracking my brain while I looked for clues I noted a lack in his usual masculine confidence. Normally Gibson exuded his alpha male trait without even being aware of it. I couldn't allow myself to think too hard about that because my confidence was easily dented when it came to loving a man like Gibson.

Our mood must have been more overt than we thought because

Piper slid her chair back and began putting the plates in a pile on top of hers.

"Leave it, honey. Gibson and I will do it. Go relax in the den we'll be in there shortly."

"Actually, I'm pretty tired, Chloe, if you don't mind I'm going to get an early night. I haven't been sleeping that well, but I think tonight I just may be able to do that."

Gibson stood and stepped away from his chair rounded the table and pulled her into a hug. Leaning back he looked at her with affection. "I know it's really tough for you right now. Tomorrow we'll get some plans together and at least you'll be able to form some kind of routine. It'll help to know what's coming day to day until you feel more in control of your feelings."

Seeing the way she had the confidence to sag against his chest was important. It made me understand how clear her dependence was on us and how Gibson's words had comforted her. Scraping my chair back against the wooden floor I stood and stepped forward. Piper left Gibson's arms and walked into mine.

Piper squeezed me tightly. I heard her swallow hard before she pulled back and gave me a watery smile. Her mouth quivered as her tears brimmed and in barely a whisper she muttered, "Thank you." I patted her back, releasing her from my hold as both Gibson and I stood quietly as she left the kitchen.

The second she'd gone Gibson began clearing the table and I placed my hand over his. "No. Later. Whatever it is you have to tell me I want to know now."

Looking solemnly into my eyes Gibson swallowed, nodded slowly and closed his eyes. When he opened them again he took a deep breath, grabbed my hand tight and led me into the great room. Spinning me slowly into position he sat down gently on the sofa with me.

From the way he'd taken care to make me comfortable I knew the news was bad. His gesture fueled my apprehension. Panic rose in my chest and the only thing that helped me was whatever he had to say was difficult for him.

"Chloe, darlin' you know how much I love you, right? I'll never give you cause to question that." Gibson usually never cared about tact when he had something to say. He'd always been forthright and unfiltered, especially when he was frustrated or angry about something and that was definitely the vibe he was giving me at the time. Instead of reassuring me the way he was struggling to tell me and the way he was treading carefully only made me fear the worse.

Chapter Four

THE MOMENT OF RECKONING

Gibson

ANY OTHER TIME STARING INTO CHLOE'S BEAUTIFUL BIG INKY BLUE eyes would have made me hard. Not that day. I was choked because there was no understanding of how she'd take the news I had to offer. My life's path appeared to follow a series of flukes and being at that concert and noticing that woman and child in a crowd of almost ten thousand people was obviously meant to be. There was no way around what I had to do so I prayed for support and hoped for the best.

"Darlin' I have no idea how to tell you this ..." She swallowed nervously, and my chest tightened. I realized I was holding my breath and released it slowly. She did the same as I saw her trying to maintain her dignity. It was one of the reasons I loved Chloe she always appeared to accept things in the first instance and think deeper at her leisure. She wasn't the jump-off-the-deep-end dramatists like most of the women I usually attracted.

"Just say it, Gibson, you're scaring me," she snapped, breathing deeper again for control as she fidgeted with her wedding ring.

"Please Chloe...fuck!" I spat back then growled because I didn't want to say the words I felt would destroy her. I ran my hands through my hair and stared intensely at her while she looked at me and stilled her hands. Then she stayed still and sat staring directly back, waiting to hear what I had to say.

"Last night at the gig I had a visitor." Breaking eye contact I looked down at my shoes and ran my hand through my hair. *Fuck.*

"And?" she prompted for me to keep going.

I raised my head and slumped lower beside her. My hand smoothed over the silky skin on her shoulder and I placed a small kiss there. I reached for her hand and smoothed my thumb over her tiny knuckles in a soothing gesture.

"A woman in the audience caught my eye—" Chloe immediately pulled her hand out of mine and turned to stand but I caught her around her waist and held her down beside me. I couldn't take it if she'd rejected me. "No, Chloe I didn't cheat. That's not what this is. I think you know me better than that."

"Did Morgan come to see you? Was it her?" Morgan was the one woman who almost rocked the boat for us. She'd been my friend before I got with Chloe but she turned out to be a piece of work. For a long time I didn't twig but dropped her like a stone after I saw the games she played around my girl.

"It has nothing to do with Morgan. I know how you feel about her. I'd never let her interfere with us in any way." She continued to look at me with a worried expression and it had been hard enough trying to think of how to break the news to her, but with her right there in front of me it felt like the last thing in the world I wanted to tell her. Seconds passed where I felt the weight of my news until I took a deep breath and held her hands.

"Listen, I've been thinking about this all night and for most of the day before I got here and there's no easy way to say what I have to tell you, darlin'. I wish with my whole heart there was so I figure the best thing I can do is be honest. I'm just gonna string it out there for you and we'll take it from there, but remember how much I love you."

Chloe tensed in my arms like she was bracing herself and turned her head away from me. "Last night I found out I'm a dad," I said in a flat tone like it would somehow lessen the impact of my words.

Turning her face to look at me her eyes met mine. Instantly the light left them as an expression of total destruction washed over her face. Watching the effect of my words was soul destroying as her body instantly compressed several inches in defeat and I saw the vein in her neck pulse rapidly. She was in shock.

"A...a dad? You're a father?" she repeated in a small hurt voice. Averting her gaze she stared up at the mountain tops and twilight sky from the huge bank of windows and sat motionless. Tears glistened and my heart cracked in two. A dim light in the room came from the fire in the fireplace and usually, I loved to watch her by the glow of the fire but not with the wounded look she had in her eyes.

Quietly I sat as she absorbed what I'd said and held on desperately to the fact we loved each other. I had no doubts we'd get through the situation, but I didn't expect our future to be easy. My faith in Chloe was strong and I was confident she'd eventually deal with the situation neither of us could change, with grace.

After a few moments her fingertips moved to her temples as she drew small circles on her skin and still I waited as the rest of her body language displayed her struggle to assimilate the information I'd given her.

When she'd gathered her thoughts, she turned her head to look at me. The pain in her eyes told me my news had cut her to the bone. Bravely she straightened her back and swallowed awkwardly fighting back tears. When she looked up at me her normally bright eyes were red rimmed but she offered me a sad smile.

"Congratulations," she whispered as her lips quivered before she leaned forward and pressed them to mine. Her humility wasn't the response I'd expected, but I wasn't surprised. It was Chloe's way to push aside her own feelings to consider mine at a time when the news I had given another woman a child must have been killing her.

"I'm sorr—" before I could apologize she pressed her soft fingertips to my dry lips to silence me. I was distracted by a lump in my throat at how easy she was making it for me.

"Please, don't do that, Gibson. I ... it's okay. I'm okay. This was just ... unexpected." She swallowed roughly a couple of times like she was choking back tears. "I'll do better, I just need some time," she said bravely as tears began to flow despite her reassurance. One fell from her lashes and I had no hesitation in kissing it from her cheek in an automatic reaction.

In that moment my chest tightened so much I thought I'd never breathe again. I'd blown up her world as she knew it and I'd have done anything not to hurt her.

"Boy or girl?"

"A girl."

Chloe smiled sadly and nodded, as fresh tears fell when I answered. She'd always wanted a girl.

This was heartbreaking to watch. I'd had the previous twenty-four hours to think about this and my head was reeling from the news, along with the impromptu introduction to my daughter. It had still felt unreal that I had little girl who had been on this Earth for the previous six and a half years and I'd had no idea.

Jonny my driver, pilot, bodyguard, was one of my closest friends. I had spoken to him before he'd flown me back home to Colorado the morning after the gig. I'd had time to think although my mind was set on replay to the brief meeting with the little girl I fell in love with as soon as she had spoken. Her voice was cute—lyrical, and her name was perfect. Melody.

For as long as I live I'll never forget the moment I walked into that room and her little bright inquisitive eyes connected with mine. A wide beaming smile spread over her face in instant recognition of me and my heart immediately opened to her.

"My mommy said you sing really well and she was right. She says I take after you with my music." She'd said. Despite the fact there had been no formal introduction to me as her dad she had spoken to me with the same confidence my mom had instilled in me.

"What's your name precious?" I asked, gently.

"Melody," she responded confidently and my heart caught in my throat. She was perfect and she took my breath away.

"Well Melody thank you for your kind praise for my singing, sweetheart. It means the world to me." I instantly loved her.

"That's okay, I'm not making it up. If you stank I'd tell you." Her comment made me chuckle and I glanced at her mom who was watching Melody with pride.

"You think I can ask Len my drummer to show you how to strike a beat while I talk with your mom a little?"

"Sure. I play the drums in school sometimes, but guitar is my favorite instrument." I called Len to come in and asked him to take her on stage for five minutes while I spoke to her mom.

"I wish you'd told me," I said to Kiran after Len had closed the door.

"And I'd have been thought of as another hoax until my name had been dragged through the mud. You think I'd have wanted that for her? It was bad enough I behaved the way I did with you that night and I've gone over it a thousand times in my head why I did. I'd never thrown myself at any man the way I did with you. I must have lost my mind. For I don't know how long afterward I hated myself."

I felt ashamed because she probably would have been shunned and she'd made it sound like she was really a nice girl. I didn't recognize her mother but before I met Chloe I was a dog. It was only when she told me where we'd met a fleeting hazy memory formed in my mind. Fortunately Lennox had taken Melody to see the instruments on stage during that part of the conversation.

Kiran was a stripper and I'd never have met her if Len and the boys in M3rCy hadn't dragged me to a strip joint that night. I was fully tanked on gin, she was hot for me, and the rest is history.

She'd had never sought me out for child support and had been taking care of Melody all by herself, and said she had no intention of hitting me up for anything apart from the chance for Melody to know who her father was as she'd become more inquisitive over the previous year.

As our conversation went on Kiran told me Melody was showing the same aptitude for musical knowledge that I had and when she saw I was playing close to home she figured it was the one chance Melody may have to know her father.

Kiran went on to tell me she'd taken the job after she and her mom had been evicted by a rogue landlord. They'd been sleeping in Kiran's mom's station wagon until three days before I saw her performance. They'd been living paycheck to paycheck when they found themselves locked out with no notice. They had needed cash fast and was so desperate she'd walked into a local strip club and was hired on the spot.

"Tell me about her. What is she like?" We had both sat in a prolonged period of silence each with our own thoughts when Chloe interrupted my memories of what Kiran had told me.

"I don't want to hurt you, Chloe and I don't want any of this to come between us, but she's my daughter—"

"Gibson, I'm trying. It's just... so sudden. I need time to get my head around it, you know? The only thing I'm sure of right now is that I never want you to feel you can't see her or talk about her because of me."

The deep sigh that left my throat was for two reasons. Relief she felt that way and shame for the hurt I was causing her. "Until yesterday we were childless, except for the commitment we just made to Piper. My one regret about us is that I never—"

"You can cut that the fuck out right now, darlin', I won't have you feeling inadequate. I'm more than happy that it's just the two of us—"

"But that's just it, Gibson. It isn't anymore." The look of apprehension and uncertainty that passed through her eyes broke my heart.

"So what do we do? Tell me how to deal with this? I want a relationship with my daughter but I don't want that to wreck what we've got," I replied as my eyes searched her face.

"What's her mother like?" Chloe sounded calmer than I expected.

"She appears nice enough, I don't know I wasn't really paying much attention to her. I was kinda focused on the fact I had a daughter." Watching as her lips pursed together I waited for the next question.

"What does she look like?"

"Mom. She looks like my mom. I took some pictures, here," I replied nervously and swiped my cell phone screen.

Chloe huddled around me and laid her head on my shoulder while she stared at the face of the cute little girl I could never deny was mine. A small gasp left Chloe's mouth and I knew she saw what I saw.

Melody's eyes were so similar to mine it was like looking into a mirror. Chloe slid her hand underneath mine as I held the phone as she continued to stand quietly beside me. I slowly flicked through the few pictures I'd taken until I heard her sniff.

My heart tore in half crushed from hurting my beautiful wife in this way while the other half sang with joy because I felt something I never thought I would—the love a parent has for their child.

"Come here, darlin'," I coaxed. I dropped my cell phone onto the sofa before I grabbed her by the waist and scooped her up into my lap. Climbing onto my legs I could see how hard she was trying to be brave, but the shock of what I'd just told her and the fact our lives had changed forever must have been crippling her with pain. The tension in her body made her feel stiff in my arms.

"We'll take it slowly, darlin'," I said sounding more confident than I felt. Chloe was truly crushed by my news and I understood why. The best of the best in fertility clinic doctors and all the fancy hi-tech treatments had failed us. Not to mention all the physical and emotional pain she'd gone through in an effort to give us a child of our own. I was certain she'd accept Melody at some point but I hated the fact she had to go through the pain of acceptance to get there.

Chloe pulled away from me and stood up straight. Adjusting the hem of her red cotton top she glanced down, her eyes instantly connecting with me. A small rueful smile formed on her lips. "I'll be okay, Gibson. We'll be okay. I need a little time...to adjust," she said with a shrug.

Deep down I knew I'd have to make Chloe feel secure and nurture her with love to make her feel secure. I knew I'd lost a lot of ground on that with my news. I had to do that because there was no way I'd allow Melody to drive a wedge between us.

I stood up and faced her, grabbed her hair, and pushed her face toward me from behind. I held her inches from my face and placed her hand over my heart. "No matter what, Chloe, you are mine. Feel that beat? It's yours. You are my heart. Nothing is going to change that. I won't let anything come between us. I know you don't want to hear it but I am sorry this has happened. Six and a half years ago means she was conceived right before we got together. Her pregnancy dates were within weeks of me arranging to meet you. I thought I'd put my legacy behind me but I guess my past was bound to catch up with me at some point."

Knowing Chloe the way I did I knew it didn't take much to dent her confidence after the history she'd been through and how important it was to keep her close. I felt if I gave her space and time she'd ask for more and before I knew it we'd have a fight on our hands to get what we have back.

I wrapped my arms tightly around her letting the warmth of my body seep onto hers. In the embrace between us I had wanted her to feel the remorse I felt for her situation. Chloe willingly accepted my gesture and melded against me, absorbing my affection. Rubbing her back to sooth her wasn't anything new so she relaxed into my arms and let me take care of her.

"Let's go to bed the dishes can wait," I said because it was me who felt insecure in that moment.

"Okay," she whispered knowing we both needed to feel close to each other. My heart swelled with love at how compassionate she was being.

Dipping my knees I scooped her up into my arms and took the wooden steps to the upper floor two at a time. "I really missed you, darlin'," I mumbled into her hair as I held her tightly, "did you miss me?" I asked in a question I usually asked her each time I came home after traveling without her.

"Like you wouldn't believe," she answered honestly despite all the turmoil she must have felt. I swallowed hard and focused on her soft curves in my arms and thanked God for her gentle nature.

Most women would have thrown a fit and kicked me out on the street with the news I had brought home, and they'd have taken me for every penny they could get. But they weren't my Chloe. She came from a special breed and even though it killed me to have this happen to her I knew we'd deal with it together.

Chapter Five

STUNNED

Chloe

For a split-second I thought I'd misheard him, then when I looked at the pain in his eyes I knew I hadn't. It was real. Gibson had a child. Initially I felt numb—stunned, right before I was overwhelmed by a torrent of emotions flowing through my mind and body. Each individual feeling conflicted with the last inside my head as waves of sadness, guilt, and defeat washed over me.

Looking into the eyes of the man I loved most in this world, the man who held me like he'd never let me go was painful. I drew a deep breath and reminded myself no matter what life threw at us, a love like ours didn't happen every day. Then I wondered in doubt if I deserved the kind of love a man my Gibson gave me.

Reluctantly I'd taken a chance on Gibson when my head had been screaming no. It was the best advice I'd ever ignored from myself. Since we'd been together the love and trust we had in each other had and breathed new life into me. Each year that passed had gotten better than the last and he'd done everything in his power to make my life complete. Most of the time my cup was full, but every now and again I became consumed by the one thing I felt neglectful to have given in return.

Remembering everything we'd been through made my chest

tighten in distress. There was never even false hope of a natural pregnancy. I was never even a day late yet in my menstrual cycle yet I used to spend a fortune on pregnancy kits— convinced every time we'd made love that time it would be a success.

Flashbacks of praying for two small lines on a stick shot through my mind but my prayers were never answered. Gibson never complained even though he had the indignity of jerking off into a cup. After two rounds of IVF treatment I felt even more of a failure when I only managed to produce two eggs on the second attempt.

When I got the call to come back, only one had become impregnated in the petri dish, but like Gibson joked we only needed one. By some miracle it took and we celebrated quietly, delighted in the hope of becoming parents late in the fall. Sadly it wasn't to be and I miscarried our only chance of a child of our own; my precious baby, at twelve weeks and one day—just when we thought we were out of the woods.

After long discussions with our fertility experts they informed us that with no viable options to have a biological child the only course left open to us was egg donation or adoption. Gibson firmly drew a line by saying if we couldn't make a baby together we'd accept we weren't supposed to be parents.

The pragmatist in him reasoned with all the charity work he already did it would be impossible to pick a handful of kids from the ones he supported when adoption was mentioned so we decided our lives would be fulfilled by caring for others.

For a rock star who'd lived life on the edge before he met me, he was a huge humanitarian and spent many hours a week making deals with the overseas development offices and it was my knowledge of the extent which he went to for them that helped me accept his word when he stated he was happy for it to be just the two of us at home.

The way Gibson told me about his daughter was done with sensitivity for my previous heartache. Yet he remained the honest man I expected him to be. Empathetic to us as a couple and careful of my feelings, he trod carefully but didn't sugar-coat anything about our new circumstances.

Inside my soul hurt because I felt the restraint Gibson had because he was torn. He felt unable to show his happiness about Melody for fear it would crush me. He should have known I was already crushed anyway because of my own failings and I wished he had just allowed his emotions to flow freely.

Separately, I had another set of thoughts running through my mind because I felt gutted someone else had easily managed what I had tried so very hard to do. Despite the fact I couldn't give him a child he had one anyway. Deep down I knew after all we'd been through he should have been celebrating his child's life no matter how she got here.

Gibson was this outspoken alpha male but with me he had always been caring and gentle. Most women would have given him a dreadful time for disclosing his news, but they weren't me. But I felt no one knew Gibson like I did. Guilt ridden, he wrapped his warm arms around me and swept me tight to into chest. Lifting me up he carried me to bed and regardless of what was happening in our life— I let him.

Many wives would have been distraught to be in my position but I'd have been selfish to deny him the joy I knew a child would bring him. Also, why would I reject any child of my husband's when we'd tried desperately to have a child of our own? Gibson placed me gently on the bed and pressed his hands into the mattress either side of him.

"Know this, Chloe Barclay. Melody's mother means nothing to me. Obviously, she's the mother of my baby, but that's where the connection ends. There are no feelings for her—not even anger that she kept Melody from me for all of this time."

In a voice laced with determination I knew he wanted me to believe it, and I did. Another wave of emotion hit me with the thought I had stuck in my brain. Seven years I'd been with Gibson—five trying to have his child. For every day we had poured love into that one thing I failed. Yet all it had taken for Melody's mom to have Gibson's child was a meaningless fuck with a rock star.

Life is unfair. Tears trickled sideward from my eyes to my ears as I lay on my back looking up at my man. The injured eyes looking back were dull. Gibson's will to fight for me was almost palpable in our bedroom and it was easy to see the agony he felt for me.

Crawling up the bed he spooned into me, his huge warm arms cradling me into his chest and the warmth from his body comforting me. He sighed deeply and exhaled a long slow breath. "Please don't cry, darlin'. I never meant to hurt you. I'm so fucking sorry it has to be like this."

"I know."

"Yeah?"

"Yeah. I don't care that you have a child, Gibson. If she's yours—she's mine. B...but I just wish I..."

His arms tightened around me and he gave me three tighter squeezes like he felt desperate, "I know, darlin', but maybe we can build what we got around the kids we've been given. Piper and Melody both need good parents. I know Melody's got a mom but the girl needs support with my daughter. From what she says she's working two jobs and my daughter still sleeps in the same bed as her."

"Really?"

"Yep, three generations in one household. Let's be clear on this right from the get-go, Chloe. Like I said before I have no feelings toward that woman and have never had a relationship with Melody's mom. It was purely a one night stand that she regrets, but you know me, I have to take care of what's mine."

"It's one of the reasons we're together, Gibson. I wouldn't expect anything less."

I started to move and his arms went slack to allow me. Shuffling around to face him, I stared up into his concerned eyes with a soul-searching look knowing instinctively what I had to do. "I want to meet her."

"Yeah?" he asked, moving his head back a little to see my face.

"You'd rather I didn't?" I asked cocking my eyebrow in disbelief. Gibson stood staring back and didn't speak.

"That's what I thought. But first we need to talk to Piper and get her settled. After that as soon as we can make the situation we've all fallen into feel normal, the better the possible outcome all round."

Inhaling sharply he leaned forward and pressed a kiss to my lips. "Chloe darlin' you have no idea what a saint you are. You've no idea how much you mean to me. Most days I don't stand a chance to love you less 'cause you do or say something that makes me fall a little bit deeper. I know what's happened isn't ideal and it isn't how either of us would have wanted this, but I can't help but see her as a gift and—she's here." Gibson's eyes pleaded and I picked my words carefully.

"Look, I know I'm upset and I'm sorry. I wish I could just have been happy for you. I mean I *am* happy for you. Truly I am. It's just... after everything we've been through this is hitting a little hard, you know? If I thought crying unconsolably would make a difference I'd probably be doing that right now but it won't." His eyes winced but he didn't stop looking at me.

"No, I need to be logical about this. I knew about your past when I got with you. Your legacy with women has been in my face since the first time I met you."

"I was young, free, and single—" I placed my hand to his lips again.

Our relationship had always felt too good to be true. My hotter-than-hell rock star had a clean slate in terms of marriages, relationships, and kids—until now. Finding out there was a child after all this time was a shock, but reacting badly would never change the outcome. Melody was Gibson's child and I was her step mom so I couldn't deny it either. It just meant I'd work harder for her acceptance.

"She's a sweet kid, Chloe. From what I've seen I don't reckon she'll make it hard work for you. The way she just took to me was so natural and—" His voice was soft but he suddenly stopped because he'd begun to get caught up in the excitement. I could hear his affection for her; it was already there in his voice when he spoke about her.

I was surprised by my lack of envy and found it ironic that this should have happened. No matter what my own personal turmoil I wanted him to have a close relationship with Melody. He'd already missed so much.

My initial reaction would always set the scene for how Gibson regarded his child so I managed it the best way I knew how. I didn't want him to feel awkward when I was around them. Once I had reconciled that point in my mind I felt like I could breathe deeply for the first time since I'd found out about her.

Rolling me onto my back Gibson climbed over me, caging me in with all four limbs.

"Babe, I can hear you thinking again. And I know what you're saying. But I gotta tell you, darlin', you're my everything. You got me?

We've been through so much and come out of the other side stronger for it. This isn't going to come between us, darlin'. You gotta trust me on that, understand?"

"I do, and it won't. I love you with my whole heart, Gibson. I trust you to do the right thing and as we're being honest I'll tell you if I'm being frozen out or if I don't agree with something. If I speak to you, I'll expect you to listen and not wave it aside."

A frown creased Gibson's brow as he stared down with a serious face. "I'd never wave what you had to say aside."

"Yeah but your daughter wasn't in the picture then. Just remember emotions can run high when kids are in the mix that's all I'm saying."

"Promise I'll hear you out," he said with conviction as his eyes searched my face. I could tell by the look Gibson gave me he was done talking. Leaning forward he brought his face down to mine. Pressing his lips to the corner of my mouth he murmured, "Do you remember the first time I took you?"

I stared up at him because I was still suffering from the trauma of an abusive relationship when we got together. "Yes," I whispered and a jolt of electricity ran from my head to my core at the sudden image that flashed through my mind with his unexpected question. No matter how much I'd been in turmoil that day when he took me he'd made me feel safe.

"What did you ask me?"

"I asked you to show me how you could make me feel."

"You did and can you remember what I asked in return?"

"You asked me to trust you," I replied remembering a time that trust was difficult for me. Nevertheless, I gave it to him.

"Do you trust me now?"

"I do because you came straight to me as soon as you knew about Melody. You could have held on to this for a while until you'd figured it out, but you didn't."

"I'm asking you to trust me again now. Can you do that? See this?" hovered above me taking his weight on one arm and gestured between us, "I need this closeness with you, Chloe. I need you. When you're not with me I miss you so fuckin' badly," he whispered and dropped his hand to the mattress again.

Peppering tiny kisses over my face and down my neck, he murmured, "Trust me, darlin', I got you." Sliding his one knee between my legs then the other he sat back on his heels and studied me.

Reaching out to me he swept his huge hands lightly down my arms I shivered under his touch and he smiled. "I love how responsive you are to me, darlin'." When he reached my waist, he traced his hands along the hem of my cotton top and slid his warm palm inside. It glided it over my stomach. My nipples pebbled under his touch as his callused fingertips reached them through my lacy bra. Involuntarily my head rolled from side to side in ecstasy as his mouth migrated back to my neck.

"C'mere," he demanded pulling me up into a sitting position when his hand snaked under my back. Seconds later he'd stripped my top over my head then every garment of clothing followed in quick succession.

As he dropped the last item on the floor his eyes raked hungrily over me. "Fuck. Look at you," he whispered in a voice laced with emotion then growled a little as his hands landed on both my shoulders. Once again he trailed them lightly down both arms all the way down to my hands. Shivers and electricity flowed through every fiber in my body.

Gibson and I always felt better as soon as our bodies were linked together. No matter what else went on in our lives our passion and need for each other was rock solid.

As his hands reached mine he took one and turned it palm up. Dipping his head toward my upturned hand he laid a soft slow, almost reverent kiss at the center. My eyes followed his head as he lifted it again and fixed to his.

My heart slowed right down when I saw the look he gave me because it carried a thousand apologies for making my heart ache. No words could have said what he had with that look. I licked my lips and swallowed back the emotion rising into my throat because I knew part of him would move mountains for me. Then again, I knew he'd move mountains in the future to keep the child he'd always wanted to have.

As I stepped back to put one foot on the floor Gibson pulled my hand forward making me lift myself onto the other elbow to see what he was doing. With a serious look on his face he placed the flat of my palm against the front of his jeans. "Feel that? That's all for you. Always only for you. No-one makes me as hard as you do, darlin', and there isn't a woman out there who has ever made my heart race the way it does when I'm with you.'"

For all the women Gibson had been with, as far as I knew, he'd been faithful to me. His heart was pure in his love and I believed him when said he didn't want anyone else. I smiled as I slowly swept my hand over the solid ridge between his hips before my fingers mapped out the long thick definition inside his jeans.

My fingertips curled around him as best as I could and I pressed my hand firmer against him. My mouth was dry as I glanced back up to look at him. A smile played on Gibson's lips but the dark look in his eyes threatened pure carnal lust. Silent seconds passed as his breathing became heavy and I realized he was barely restraining himself.

All the while my fingers and thumb traced the outline of his dick under the denim Gibson stood watching, first what I was doing, then gave me a stare full of lust. My pussy juice pooled between my legs as my need for him became overwhelming. I reached for his belt but his hand clamped firmly over mine and he shook his head.

"Nah, I want to eat you out. Tonight I need to show you just how much you mean to me, darlin' and if you don't mind I wanna take my own sweet time with this delicious body of yours. I'm gonna taste every fucking inch of you—twice. And when you think I'm done— I'll just be getting started. Trust me, Chloe. I'm gonna fuck you hard and you're gonna ride my dick to the moon because I never want you to forget what we have."

I expected to see a roguish smile accompanying such a bold statement from him but I his face was stoic and that told me he was worried. Claiming my body was his way of demonstrating I was irreplaceable.

Pushing me back down on the bed he grabbed my thighs from under my knees and pulled me down the edge of the bed. The comforter came with me bunching under my back. The unevenness of the material only made the rough way he handled me more exciting. He dipped his nose and ran it along my seam inhaling deeply.

"Fuck. You smell like heaven," he muttered before licking his lips and placing his tongue on my clitoris. Sparks of ecstasy radiated throughout my nervous system. Straight away his eyes raked over my body, up to my face, and looked into mine. "Damn, darlin', this never gets old," he said then concentrated on jabbing his tongue in and out of my entrance before sucking with force. White heat spread feelings of pleasure throughout my veins.

My hands automatically tangled in his hair as my back arched while I tried to writhe in sweet torture at the way he flicked my clit and explored my entrance. It didn't take me long before I felt the heat from his expert attention he paid with his mouth.

As soon as Gibson felt my legs start to shake he clamped his hands tighter around my thighs and pinned me to the bed. Feeling pleasure as it built higher a small squeal tore from my throat and was immediately followed by the onslaught of an earth-shaking orgasm that almost stopped my heart. Shaking and squirming I tried to break free of his grasp as he lapped and sucked relentlessly until I rode my orgasm out.

Chapter Six

GETTING CLOSE

Gibson

CHUCKLING HEARTILY, I SMACKED HER ASS SHARPLY, PUSHED MYSELF off the floor, and stood up. The loud crack from my hard palm on her firm soft skin echoed through the bedroom. Chloe's mouth formed a silent O in shock but she was still trying to come back down after I'd made her come hard.

"That was a neat little warm up gig, darlin'. Are you ready for the headliner?" I joked, smiled wickedly, and reached for my belt buckle. Chloe moaned and closed her legs and I immediately stopped what I was doing. "No, I want to see your pussy. Put your feet together and draw them up to your ass then let them relax." I snapped, firmly. Immediately, her lust drunk eyes darkened as she complied with my demand.

Despite her history Chloe loved when I controlled her in the sack. I wasn't an easy lay in that I didn't just lie there and let her ride me, I was pretty athletic in bed and she'd learned to cope with my firm handling and stamina. I knew what she needed instinctively. As soon as Chloe gave her trust in me she relaxed into our sexual relationship.

To look at her I'd never have thought she was the kind of girl who liked having her hair pulled or her throat squeezed when I fucked her, but she did. The first time I wrapped my hand around her throat she grabbed it, clawing it away with both hands. I felt like shit because I'd just got lost in the moment and hadn't considered her history.

Afterward we talked about it but she was insistent she had to get over it because I liked it, and she wasn't allowing the guy who had shattered her faith in men to win. Gradually, she gave me all of her trust and since then we'd never looked back.

As soon as I spoke Chloe's huge brown eyes snapped to look at mine to give me her full attention as she followed my strict instruction. My eyes perused her beautiful endless curves as she lay there buck naked with her legs spread wide at the knee like the wings of a beautiful butterfly.

The low sound of rustling material and metal broke the silence as I shed my belt and shoved my jeans roughly down my legs. Chloe watched intently and my dick grew thicker when I saw her eyes concentrated on me. Shoving them over my hips I felt the ache as my heavy balls dropped between my legs and my thick solid cock sprang directly toward her like some kind of homing device. It pointed straight at her entrance as my eyes became riveted to the glistening wet inner lips of her pussy.

Every nerve in my body urged me to fuck her dirty. I wanted that more than anything, but it wasn't about taking pleasure it was about giving it; it was about worshiping her body because Chloe deserved to know that no child could replace what she was to me.

Without taking my eyes from her petals of sensitive skin between her legs I toed one shoe off and then the other pulling each foot free of my jeans as I did so. Once I was naked I tilted forward on the bed and couldn't help placing my mouth and tongue between her legs again. From the very first moment I had tasted Chloe I knew I never wanted to put my mouth on another woman again.

Whenever she let me between her thighs I became lost in the effect of what the woman did to me. Her smell, taste, the feel of her soft velvety creases, how she moaned softly and screamed in delight, but most of all the look she gave me when she came. She was my perfect match.

Pure but not, experienced but not, a whore in bed, but only for me.

Chloe was exactly what my life had been missing. I knew it the first time she slid down my dick.

Arching her back, Chloe pushed her pussy into my face as her hips began to gyrate with need, half of me wanted her to come on my tongue but my dick dripped with precum and the ache in my balls couldn't be ignored. In several quick moves I'd taken her calves in my palms and rotated her legs up to her chest. Chloe breathed hard and fast, unable to hide the anticipation of what I had been about to do. Her head rolled to the side.

"Look at me," I commanded as I grabbed my stiff dick in my hand and dragged the wet tip down her slit. "What do you want, Chloe?" I goaded.

"You," she whispered.

"How do you want me?"

"However you want to take me," she murmured as I stared with intent.

"Fast or slow, darlin', what's your desire?"

"You're my desire, Gibson. Don't overthink it just give it to me."

I chuckled because her response was cheesy and was rewarded with a pretty little smile. My hand left my dick as both grabbed her tits and squeezed them tight. A soft gasp left Chloe's mouth as her head tilted and sunk deeper into the mattress. The breaths we shared became hot, shallow, and fast in anticipation.

She was my dream vision in my sexual fantasies and I loved watching her like that. Every fiber in her body was at work as it vibrated in anticipation. I quickly put one nipple in my mouth and rolled my tongue around the pebbled hard bud. A gasp tore from her lips when I slowly nibbled on one.

I knew every square inch of her body and how she'd react depending on where my hands, tongue, mouth or cock touched her. Chloe was like the finest tuned guitar and responded fluidly to which-ever direction I desired to rain pleasure on her.

When she was ready to take me in her legs widened, left their posi-tion and wrapped tightly around my waist before she angled herself to make contact with my dick. I felt her ankles lock the pressure from her heels as she pulled me closer. As soon as her nails dug into my back my cock jumped in protest and I dropped to my elbows at each side of her head.

"What do you want, Mrs. Barclay. Say it. Talk dirty to me," I said with a grin and felt I was pushing my luck considering the news she'd just been given.

"I want you inside me," she said in a serious tone.

"My fingers, my tongue? What do you want?" I asked teasing my wet tip back and forth as she arched her ass up toward me in her pathetic attempt to take me in.

"Please slide your thick hard cock inside me. I want to feel you close." My forehead dropped to hers.

"You're the love of my life, darlin'," I whispered seductively as I stopped at the lips of her pussy and began to glide inside. Chloe's breath hitched as did mine at the heady sensation of our bodies joining. The pressure from all sides squeezed my dick tight and for a second it was almost enough to make me come. I stilled letting my wife catch her breath then I drew back a little and slid deep again to allow her time to adjust.

"God, you're beautiful," I muttered as my mouth found her neck and I sucked on her skin. A rash of goosebumps spread at the sensation as Chloe's ass began to undulate underneath mine.

"Is this enough? Is this all you want?" I goaded, anticipating how swiftly she became frustrated at the pace I was moving into her.

"No, I want more," she said in a desperate tone her teeth nibbling into my shoulder.

"I'm not convinced darlin'. You're gonna have to persuade me that what I'm giving you isn't all you need."

Suddenly she scored her nails down my back and dug them into my ass her pussy grinding on my pubic bone. My reaction was purely carnal. Sliding my hands between her and the mattress I held her tightly as I rolled myself onto my back. Chloe's eyes darkened with lust as she swept her hair to the side and dropped her head to suck on my neck. "Fuck. How hard do you want it?" I asked in a low voice full of intent.

"All that you have," she whispered like some kind of challenge.

"Oh, darlin', don't tempt me, I'd fuck this pussy raw in a heartbeat tonight to show you how much I need you."

"Don't you think that's just what I need?" she whispered as she sat up straight taking me balls deep inside. Placing her hands on my chest she began to ride me at a pace I'd rarely seen. Completely taking charge like she was laying claim to my body. She should have known she didn't have to do that, I was already hers.

At that second her desperation came through and I felt the vulnerability she'd tried so hard to hide during our conversation. I knew immediately if I didn't give her my all right then and there it would have left her with doubts she'd have harbored forever regarding her place now that we knew Melody existed.

Grabbing her possessively by the hips I spread my legs for greater traction and dug my heels into the mattress then fucked her from below like some demon who was possessed. Chloe's high-pitched scream filled the room in less than a minute as her orgasm crushed my dick tight, deep inside her pussy. My hand left her hip and gripped her neck pulling her mouth to mine as I silenced her cries of ecstasy.

Feeling her body tremble in mine, I folded my arms across her back to make her feel safe while she rode herself back from the edge. Less than a minute later I did it again, and a third time until she begged me to stop, seconds later I let myself go slamming into her hard and allowing a low grunt to fall from my throat as I spurted my seed deep inside her. Chloe's fingertips traced my eyes, nose and along my sweating hairline before they traced my lips tenderly.

"I love you with all of my heart, Gibson Barclay," she whispered and placed her soft lips firmly against mine.

"You are my heart, darlin', don't ever forget that. No matter what's going on, who's there or where my attention has to be. Up in here where no one can see, you're right there in front of me." I replied tapping my temple. Chloe smiled and dropped her head to my chest, my hand immediately cradling it and teasing her hair. "We'll get through this, darlin', and be stronger for it—just like we have everything else," I said in reassurance.

Chloe slid off me and grabbed the box of tissues from the night-stand. Normally, we did a better job of cleaning up, but that night she wiped us both down quickly and laid back beside me as if she never wanted to leave my bed. As for my own thoughts—I was glad about that because it was an indication she'd stick with me come what may. Scooping her into my side I smiled into her neck then kissed it softly before inhaling her scent one last time and closed my eyes. "Chloe?"

"Hmm?" she muttered sleepily.

"You're the very best of me," I told her.

"Yeah?"

"You are. You're the only person who's ever got me...I mean really got me. I don't care what shit comes our way, you're gonna have a fucking hard time getting rid of me, you got me?"

"Go to sleep, Gibson. I'm not going anywhere either...except maybe the spare room if you don't let me sleep. I'm exhausted and sore...and that's your fault...or maybe mine. I did ask for it, didn't I?" she rambled a little then chuckled. I snickered and kissed her hair, smoothed it down then held her tightly before I drifted off to sleep.

———

Waking to the smell of fresh perfumed body wash wasn't the worst thing in the world. Especially when the smell was on Chloe. I cracked an eye open in time to see her silent and naked form moving around the room. A slow smile spread on my lips at the vision before me.

"Now you gotta come back to bed. My wood is straining under this sheet. You can't run around naked before me and expect me to roll over and forget what I've seen."

Chloe turned to look at me and smirked as she sexily towel dried her hair and reached into her lingerie drawer for a thong. Even though I'd seen her body a thousand times my dick still twitched whenever I saw her naked. I noted her hair was half way down her back and had grown lately before an image formed in my mind of me holding her silky mane in my fist as I fucked her from behind. It did nothing to tamp my aching balls between my legs.

"Tell me, does the head on your shoulders ever win first thing in the morning or does that cock of yours control all of your waking thoughts?"

I chuckled at her remark and figured she was going to be okay after the news I brought about Melody. My heart felt lighter knowing we'd survive and deal with the implications of me having a daughter, together.

"C'mere. Don't make me beg," I said and patted the bed. My arms ached to hold her.

Stepping into the thong she teased it up her legs real slow, pulling it into place. Her hair fell forward and she looked the epitome of sexy when she stood and flicked it back over her shoulders. Her pert tits jiggled and settled on her amazing rack before she wandered over and sat down slowly beside me. I caught her off guard by gripping her roughly and swept her underneath me. We tangled in the sheet when I hovered above her but I didn't care.

"Are you teasing me?" I asked with a grin.

"Only getting ready for the day," she replied smiling up at me. Her wide grin looked anything but innocent despite her words.

"Then don't get ready, come back to bed."

"Piper?" she questioned.

My shoulders sagged a little as a deep sigh left my chest. "Shit. Yeah. Alright, I'll get dressed and come down." I offered because I knew Chloe was right we needed to think of Piper first. I relaxed my hold and rolled onto my back. "Damn, if she's gonna be a cock blocker we need to send her to college. Somewhere she can only come home when they're on breaks."

Chloe chuckled, "Yeah and what happens if there's loads of boys at college? Boys like you were, Gibson. You still think that's a good idea?"

My eyes widened because the last thing we needed in our lives at that point in time was a pregnant teen. "Fuck. Don't make this any harder than it is already, I'll have to send Jonny to live with her if there are." Chloe grinned and placed her hand behind my neck pulling my head down toward her. Giving me a slow kiss she pushed me back bit her lip like whatever she was going to say next wasn't easy.

"Let me go. Get showered and I'll make us some pancakes. We've got a daughter here we need to take care of. No doubt she's feeling very lost so we need to put our own needs aside for a bit to make sure she feels in control of her life. Can you help me do that for her, honey?"

"Yes, ma'am. I'll be down in ten," I said as she moved off the bed, pulled on a sundress and headed for the bedroom door. "but I may need to rub one out before I get down there otherwise the sweat-pant option won't be an option after all," I said. I was expecting a comment about me being crude but Chloe just rolled her eyes like I was a petulant child, bit her lip, and shook her head as she walked out the door.

"Food will be ready in twenty minutes, Gibson." Stepping out of the bedroom she closed the door quietly and I stared at the ceiling wondering what the fuck I did right to deserve her.

Chapter Seven

DETERMINED

Chloe

WHEN I WANDERED INTO THE KITCHEN I REALIZED PIPER MUST have been still in her room. I was glad for the few moments of solitude that offered me as I began to prepare pancakes and grill some bacon. My mind drifted over the previous night's conversation and although my chest tightened when I thought of what I'd learned, I knew I had to be supportive to my husband no matter how shocking his news was to me.

Life had thrown another curve ball at us and once I'd had a night to sleep on it I was determined to face it head on. Gibson wasn't perfect, I knew that when I fell in love with him. Maybe if we hadn't been through all the shit of trying to have a child of our own, I may have reacted differently to his news about Melody.

Even then, I'd like to think I was stronger than that. Not that I'd always been strong. In another life, I had been with a man I'd considered 'the one, but after the way he treated me I realized what a lucky escape I'd had.

For a long time before Gibson was in my life I'd hated who I'd become. Being with Kace had made me weak and stripped me of every shred of self esteem I had back then. That was until a few twists of fate led me to the second chance meeting and into arms of a rock star, Gibson Barclay of all people.

It wasn't my first experience of Gibson, who as a wannabe had a girl on each arm, and his tongue down another on more than one occasion when I'd seen him in the past, but the man I married was nothing like the boy he once was and I thanked God every day that he chose me to be with.

Since then I'd been through dark times and despite that his love and support had been unwavering. My incredible, beautiful, talented man not only became my best friend, my lover and my protector. He was also my rock...my everything.

If I was being honest with myself I knew the press would have a field day with Gibson's news, and the bigger picture to that would be the dirt they would dig and share with the world that as his wife I wasn't able to give him a child to make our family complete. No matter what I had to come I knew I'd have to be strong.

A complex array of emotions swept over me with that thought. Shame, sadness, sorrow, grief, and a feeling I thought I had long since became resigned to—my sense of loss. The blame lay squarely with me but Gibson had never viewed it that way and after many heart-to-heart conversations he finally convinced me I meant more to him than bringing up a child that wasn't his and mine. A feeling of irony struck me because that was exactly the position we had found ourselves in with Melody.

Continuing on autopilot with breakfast I was unaware as Piper walked into the kitchen until I caught her in my peripheral vision. I jumped, startled by her sudden presence. "Shit," I cussed as the pancake mixture slopped over the jug.

"Sorry, I didn't mean to startle you," Piper said with her hand placed over her chest. Her wide eyes looked pained as if she'd done something wrong.

I gave her a soft laugh, "No, honey, it's not your fault I was miles away," I replied as I wiped the spilt slop from the countertop with some kitchen towel.

"Smells amazing," she said, and rubbed her stomach like it ached.

"My wife always smells amazing," Gibson said, as he swept into the kitchen and grabbed my waist. He kissed me on the neck, sending shivers down my spine before he abruptly let me go and turned to Piper.

"Alright, Piper, let's talk turkey, sweetheart," he said, grabbing her hand as he pulled her toward the kitchen table. Dragging a chair out for her he nodded, "Sit, today's the first day of the rest of your life. I just want to give you a little pep talk before we move forward. You down for that?"

Piper nodded her head, a worried expression taking over as she turned to look to me for reassurance. I gave her an encouraging smile and continued to prepare breakfast. Gibson drew in a sharp breath and released it slowly, like what he had to say wasn't going to be all that palatable.

"Piper, one thing you'll get to know about me as time goes on is I'm nothing like the guy you see on T.V. I don't go around all day rocking out although there may be the occasional cussing outbreaks." Piper giggled.

"What I mean to say is I'm a man first and a rock star when I go to work, get me?" She nodded and stared nervously, her attention completely focused.

"For the past few months we've gotten to know you pretty well but I guess for you it must feel like you're stuck with a couple of strangers in this weird dream. You've been suppressed and emotionally neglected by your mom's partner for a long time, and just when you saw a way out she died. Your so goddamned pissed at the world right now. Am I right?"

"I am," she said quietly and looked down at her hands.

"Look at me, Piper. I need to see you and know you hear what I'm saying. I don't want you crying and wailing while I do this because I need you to be strong and take in what I'm about to tell you."

Instantly Piper's head snapped up her eyes darting to me then back in his direction. I finished placing the food on the plates, carried them to the table and set them down in front of them. Sliding into the seat beside Gibson I watched the innocence in Piper grab hold of his words in the same way I had once.

"I don't know if you know my background or not sweetheart but it's not particularly palatable. However, I believe it made me the man I am today. I'm rough around the edges and often misunderstood, but I'm a fierce guy to have in your corner. No one is born to be famous...unless they have famous parents already, then that's a burden. What I'm trying to say is we all start out as nothing. We are what we make of ourselves."

I sat silently and picked up my silverware slicing into my pancakes with my knife. Gibson glanced at me with a serious look on his face then gave Piper his focus again.

"My life started out as unconventional. I'm not ashamed of who I was or who I am today. Did you know I was brought up in a whorehouse?"

Watching Piper's eyes widen it was clear she had no idea about Gibson's past. Then again, she was only seventeen and Gibson had been my husband since she was ten. Most of his rags-to-riches story was water under the bridge since then.

Gibson continued, "You see, Piper, my mom did what she did to provide for me. It didn't mean she didn't love me. I never wanted for anything growing up and if anything, I had so much female love from that house it made me understand there are more important things in the world than riches or fame. Survival was key. Everyone in that house was there for their survival or that of their kids." Immediately my mind went to the families in Africa he helped to support through his charity.

"What I'm trying to say, sweetheart is I've walked in your shoes to some extent. My mom died when I was close to your age as well. Like you I had no one looking out for me but those women in that house, until I met Lennox, the drummer in our band. That guy is my brother from another mother. We'd do anything for each other."

"Since we left home I have no friends. No one to talk to about all of this."

"Of course you do, Piper, that's what I'm here for and the rest of the team," I said before taking another forkful of pancake.

Gibson picked up a piece of crispy bacon and folded it into his mouth. He chewed for a minute before washing it down with a glass of orange juice. Picking up his napkin he wiped it across his mouth and looked at Piper again.

"Chloe and I want to take care of you. We don't view this as a forced obligation. I could have set you up in a basement somewhere with a small allowance and walked away if that was my thoughts. Believe me, Chloe will tell you I can be an awkward and mean fucker if someone tries to make me do something I don't want to."

A small smile curved her lips but I could see how hard she found it to believe she hadn't just been dumped on us.

"We'll be your friends for life once you are an adult and have found your way, and by adult I don't mean eighteen. I mean when you are mentally ready to take on the challenges of being out there in the big world but until then I won't be your friend. It isn't the time to be buddies right now. You need strong and nurturing parental hands to carry you through the shit of your grief, someone to keep you safe, and guide you through the choices you're making to ensure they are sound. We want to help you achieve all you can be. Most of all you need someone to keep you straight when you're being a pain in the ass."

"What he's saying is we're here for you in all the ways you need us to be, Piper and sometimes that's not going to be pleasant. It would be easy to smother you with love and affection, to give into your whims because of your past, but that won't make you a strong woman. It'll leave you dependent on others and believe me, from experience, that's not a place you ever want to be."

Staring back with no expression I waited as she absorbed the information. She picked up her flatware and began to eat her food and for a moment I thought what we'd said was too much too soon. Gibson glanced at me and shoved some pancake into his mouth. "These are amazing, darlin', you're definitely my Goddess in the kitchen and—"

"Do you want to tell us what you think of how we see things?" I asked before Gibson had the chance to say the rest of that sentence which I presumed to be a whore in the bedroom. Gibson chuckled under his breath and continued to eat while I held Piper's gaze.

Her fork was suspended mid-air and her gaze was intense. She'd stopped chewing and swallowed the contents of her mouth before she spoke.

"I th...I think...wow." Tears filled her eyes to the brim and over-flowed. Gibson dropped his fork to his plate and swiftly moved to sit in the chair next to her.

"Fuck. Don't cry, you'll give me indigestion," he teased as a way of lightening the moment. Piper giggled through her tears and nodded wiping her eyes with her napkin and blinking rapidly.

"I'm just so confused by all that's happened but I'm really grateful to you both. You've been so kind and I don't even know you properly," she sniffed and abandoned her napkin and wiped her face with her cotton sleeve. Gibson scooped her into his chest.

"Sweetheart, I hope you know enough to know how much of a privilege it is to carry out your mom's dying wish. We see you as a gift to our home and like it or not I'm gonna see you do right by your mom. I'm determined you'll make her proud as she watches over you... as I'm sure she is right now, so eat your breakfast and let's start making some plans about how you're gonna do that, okay?"

Piper flung her arms around Gibson's neck and squeezed him tight then without speaking she dropped them and turned back to her food. Gibson glanced at me with sympathy in his eyes but winked and mouthed, "We got this, darlin'."

Gibson retook his seat next to me and began to discuss what to do next and the mood changed at the table. Gibson began to talk options and ideas and from how Piper responded it was clear she didn't want to go to college. It was obvious from her responses she'd thought a lot about what she wanted from life, but when she told Gibson she wanted to sing for a living the poor guy almost choked.

"Fuck no. It's too hard a life, Piper. Do you know how difficult it is to make a living from singing? The percentages of successful singers are less than a fraction of a percent compared to those trying to make it."

"I'll make it work. I figured I could be a wedding singer or some-thing. As long as I make enough money to live on I'll be happy," she said and poured some maple syrup on her bacon.

"Listen, teenagers have dreams like this all the time, sweetheart, but you thinking you can sing and someone else hearing what noise you make can be worlds apart. Most young girls think they can sing."

"Most aren't me. I can sing. My singing is what got me through this far. My mom taught me to sing." I could see how sceptical Gibson was and if I'm honest I was too.

"Singing at home is one thing, sweetheart it's a whole other ballgame when you're singing to a setlist, using backing tracks or music feeds."

"You don't understand, Gibson. I can sing anything I want."

"Oh course you can, Piper. But I don't think you know what I'm saying."

"You're saying I'm not good enough to make a living at it." Gibson stared her down expecting her to flinch but she didn't.

"Okay, pick a song," she insisted. My husband bit back a grin as he turned to look at me. I didn't miss how they shone with delight.

"Am I to pick a pop song you know or something I like to listen to?" he asked.

"Anything you want," she challenged.

Gibson sighed like he felt he was going to embarrass her by his choice, "Alright, Dream On," he answered.

"Aerosmith?"

Gibson looked at her in surprise, I guessed by the look on his face he never expected her to know it.

"Colin worked with them just after Aerosmith made the album that song's on. It's one of his favorites." Gibson cringed, his eyes softening.

"So... you'd rather not—"

"No you chose that song, I'll sing it," she answered, defiance in her voice.

Reaching over she grabbed her orange juice and drank it down, cleared her throat, then sat up straight tucking her hair behind her ears. Starting off softly she began to sing the words and it was immediately apparent she was doing it her way. Controlled and with the ease of a seasoned professional she began her version of the number with a confident smile.

Less than a minute later both Gibson and I were totally enthralled by the tone of her voice. Piper had serious talent. Her octave ranged widely from high to low, the tune flawless, and by the end we were speechless. Singing the last note, she sat calmly in her chair while the silence grew between the three of us.

Gibson slowly stood from his chair and walked behind her then suddenly reached down and lifted her chair with her in it and swung her around in a circle.

"Get the fuck out of here. That was so fucking sick." He shouted clearly moved and delighted by her performance. Piper smiled widely and looked as if his praise meant everything to her. Placing her chair down he slumped on the seat next to her and leaned his elbow on the table staring hypnotically at her face.

"You know how hard that song is? Apart from Steve Tyler there's maybe only a handful of people who can pull it off, but you...you were fucking effortless. The way you slid through those changes in octaves and held those long notes...damn you can sing. And that...changes everything." Before he could say what he meant his cell rang.

"Hey, Lennie," he said, pointing at Piper to stay where she was before he walked out of the kitchen to take his call. He didn't get far enough away though before I heard him say, "Yeah, I told her," I didn't need to be telepathic to know who he was talking about and my heart which had felt full just moments before, felt heavy again.

Chapter Eight

TRUST

Gibson

USUALLY LENNOX HAD MY BACK NO MATTER WHAT BUT I COULD hear from the tone in his voice he was firmly in Chloe's corner on this one. I couldn't blame him, hell I was on Chloe's side about this.

"You really told her?"

"Sure. Not like I'd hide something that monumental from her, is it?"

"I didn't mean that. I knew you'd tell her about the kid, how could you not. I just never figured you'd do it this quickly."

"We don't have secrets, Len. My whole relationship with Chloe is based on trust. I was a dog before I got with her remember?"

I was glad that Len didn't laugh when I said that because I was reminding him of the truth and how hard it was for Chloe to place her trust in me. I'd never do anything to shatter the trusting relationship between us. I once told her I'd always be truthful even if it meant hurting her and that's exactly what I'd done by telling her about Melody.

"If she knows have you arranged a date to meet her again?" He was asking if I'd figured out when Melody and Chloe could meet. Len was there toward the end of my conversation with Melody when he had brought her back from the stage. Melody asked when she could see my house and Kiran had looked to me to answer. At the time I had no clue what to say because first I knew I had to speak to Chloe and secondly any meeting would depend on how hard Chloe took the news.

"We're just sorting through Piper's shit then I'll talk to Chloe more about that. Tell Simon and Mick we'll grab dinner on Tuesday to talk through the schedule with Charlotte and feed back to Syd. I think I'm gonna need a week or two R & R while I figure my way through the latest shit storm I've created.

"Thought she was a gift?" Lennox jibed sarcastically knowing full well I didn't mean my daughter, rather the situation that came with her.

"Too fucking funny, now go sit in a corner and tug yourself off you wanker. I'll call you tomorrow when I've got a clearer picture of what's going down." Without waiting for him to answer I hung up and made my way back to the kitchen.

Piper was telling Chloe how the fuckwad that lived with her and her mom used to treat them and as I listened it became clear that her music meant everything to her in the same way as mine had with me. Even though I was staring at the innocent face of a seventeen year old the message that came from her was how much she owed to her voice and being able to escape from much of the abuse in her home due to the talent she possessed.

I felt ashamed for not believing her when she said she could sing. It wasn't a case of not believing she could— it was more a cynical attitude as to what constituted a singer in the world I lived in. My business was cut throat and die and when I looked at the petite little girl with the angelic face in front of me I could name a hundred fuckers in the business that would take her for a ride in a heartbeat. *Over my dead body.*

"Piper come here sweetheart," I said beckoning her to follow me into the great room. Piper followed with Chloe in tow. "Take a seat," I said gesturing toward the sofa. Slowly she sat, clasped her hands in her lap as her eyes searched my face for some kind of answer to what I was about to say.

Chloe made to sit beside her. "No. Here," I said sticking my hand out for Chloe to take. As soon as she did I pulled her down beside me.

Even with what was going on Chloe's needs were at the forefront of my mind.

"I owe you a big apology. I was wrong. You can sing. In fact, I'm scared you may take my job."

Piper's eyes lit up brightly and she flashed me a beaming smile. "Yeah?"

"Yeah...and you know it. No bullshit you're the bomb, I don't think I've heard a range like yours since Christina Aguilera. We gotta do something with you, sweetheart." My mind was immediately scanning my brain for the best person to mentor her.

"No. She graduates high school first, Gibson. She made a promise to her mom," Chloe said pulling us both back to reality.

"Yeah...that." I said cringing because I was getting carried away, "I agree with Chloe. Get the diploma then we can talk."

"That may take another year," Piper protested, "I've taken so much time out..."

"Then we better get you some tutors and let you get to it. I'm sure if you work hard it'll work in your favour." Nodding at Chloe to let her know we were united in that decision.

"Well now that's settled I don't want any more talk about singing until the last exam has been taken, agreed?"

I nodded my head but could see in Piper's sad dull expression she was disappointed. My heart squeezed in pity because I knew how music made me feel when I was low and Piper had to be feeling like giving up most days without it. *Parenting sucks hairy balls if this is the kinda gig they have to deal with on a daily basis.*

After a further twenty minutes of discussion it was agreed that Charlotte, my personal assistant would contact some tutoring services and Piper would remain at home during the last semester of the year.

Chloe had already been in touch with the school Principal as she already had a great relationship with her due to the other children from the families who'd attended her school short term while they'd been at the refuge. The Principal suggested Piper be affiliated to the local highschool so that she could attend the various celebrations and the prom at the end of the school year.

When Piper heard this she almost balked but Chloe said it was important that she have young people her age to relate to during her time in Colorado. After some persuasion Piper agreed and three girls were handpicked by the school Principal and arrangements were made for them to meet later that week.

Most of the morning was gone by the time we'd firmed up a plan for Piper for the following three months and I'd already considered her when Jonny and I had parted to go home. I figured Chloe and I would need some time to ourselves so I'd asked him to take Piper and show her the town.

It wasn't a big place but since she'd been at the range she'd only ever left to visit the hospital, the undertakers, and one tiny florist store. When Jonny arrived and I had told her she was being taken out I swear I saw her breathe a sigh of relief.

It must have felt good for her to find an escape after all the heavy talking we'd done that morning. I know I was and yet I knew Chloe and I weren't even close to being set with the rest of the plans we had still to face.

———

It wasn't until Piper left I realized how easily one extra person could feel like a crowd in a room when there was something important enough to discuss that I didn't want others to hear. With the opportunity for privacy I knew Chloe and I must use the valuable time to discuss the subject of Melody and when I should negotiate with Kiran to bring them to Colorado.

Glancing over at Chloe who sat flicking through a health care magazine I turned from the front door and began to walk purposefully toward her. Looking up when she heard me coming, Chloe threw the magazine carelessly onto the square wooden coffee table in front of the fire. "Shall we deal with the elephant in the room while we've got the place to ourselves?" I asked.

I sat beside her and slid my arm around her shoulders them turned her into me. "What would you prefer?"

"What do you mean?"

"What do you want me to do, Chloe? Do you want her here?

Should I bring her? Would you rather she didn't come here? What happens if her mom wants to come with her? Do I let that happen? I mean would you want your child going to people she didn't know by herself? Do I fly to Chicago for visitation? Tell me what I need to do. I didn't ask for this, but I'm responsible. It doesn't mean I can't think about your feelings and what would make it less painful for you."

"All of it is painful and nothing is, Gibson."

"What the fuck does that mean?"

"It means you do what's right for you and Melody. I don't want to be in the middle of a relationship with you and your daughter. I want you to do what you think is right for you and her. Not what's right for me. I'm incidental in your relationship. Neither Melody nor you planned it. Her mom didn't plan it either, but it is what it is. I'll accept it better if you don't pussyfoot around me and just do what you want. It'll be more natural for you both. If you start pushing everyone together it will force us apart. I hope we'll all find our happy medium in time."

Listening to her being so reasonable made me feel pissed because I knew it had to be a front and she was probably eaten alive with hurt. But if she wanted it this way then I had to accept her at her word.

"First, you are at the center of my world whether you want to be there or not. Secondly, Your happiness is very important to me, but if you insist then I'll extend an invitation to Melody and her mom here this weekend. Do you have any objections to that, darlin'?"

Turning to face me her eyes stared seriously into mine. "None. I'll make sure there's plenty of food in the pantry and that the house-keeper makes up the beds in the pool house. If you don't mind I'd rather her mom in there and not in my home. Does this woman have a partner as well?"

I cringed at Chloe's tone with regards to Melody's mother it was clear she'd be cordial but not her friend. I was pleased at that because the last thing I wanted was lines to become blurred for Melody. Nor did I want someone I'd once fucked sitting down with my wife a regular basis. "Kiran? I don't think so. Shit, I didn't ask but from how they live I wouldn't expect so."

I didn't miss the flash of annoyance that passed through Chloe's eyes when I said Kiran's name. It was one thing being the mother of my child, but when I'd addressed her so casually I'd inadvertently sparked more hurt for Chloe. Hell, I knew how it felt when I met Chloe's ex, Kace. I had wanted to gut the bastard with a rusty blade. So I could well imagine the feelings my wife had at that point in time.

I pulled Chloe into my arms and hugged her tightly. "You. Are. My. World. You Own My Soul. You got me?" Pushing slightly away, Chloe looked up into my eyes. Once again she was searching for the truth in my statement.

"For now," she whispered.

"What the fuck do you mean by that?" I challenged and gripped her wrists to stop her getting up and leaving. "You feel threatened by a child?"

"No. Not threatened by her...but it still changes the way we live our lives. I'll be supportive, Gibson. Of course I will, but don't expect me to be friends with her mother. I won't be able to do that. As soon as Melody is comfortable enough to visit on her own her mother stays at home."

"Darlin', I have to be careful what I say here because Kiran is the mother of my child, but let me just say I couldn't agree more. I practically didn't remember her at all so don't go thinking I'd run off into the sunset with my new family. You're my family. You, and now Piper and Melody, that's the order of things around here. Never be afraid I'd do anything to harm what we have."

"Then do it. Get her here. Let's get the formalities dispensed with and then we can find our balance."

I pulled her closer and kissed her forehead. "You're what matters the most, remember those words." Chloe glanced up into my eyes while a stony silence grew between us until eventually she broke the stare and moved away. "Gotta make sure the pool filter is changed and the pool house is ready. We'll need a safety net for the pool if she's coming here, Gibson."

Everything she said made perfect sense...then again, I thought everything about her was perfect, but I could hear the warning in her voice. Although Chloe had accepted the situation she was going to draw the lines around the circumstances she'd tolerate. I was glad she felt able to do that. It showed me how strong she was and how protective she'd be to keep what was hers. Me.

"I'll make the arrangements. Jonny can fly up there and bring them back," I informed her. "Meanwhile I think we should do something awesome for the rest of the day. Our time with each other is diluted to some extent so let's make sure we use it wisely. Is there anything you want to do, today?"

"Yeah. I want to be close to you. Can we go back to bed?" Chloe asked like she needed to be near me to breathe.

"Fuck, darlin', nothing would please me more." I smiled and pulled her in for a kiss, dragging her over my lap to straddle me. Chloe's pussy was directly over my hard cock and she grinned. You're such a pushover in bed you know that?" she asked and chuckled softly.

"And you're such a prick tease with that smart mouth of yours," I replied. Without hesitating I scooped her into my arms and ran up the stairs like I'd done the night before and didn't stop until I reached our bedroom.

"No gentle persuasion and tender love-making for you today, Wife. I'm gonna fuck you dirty and every which way until you can't shut your legs until at least tomorrow. And every time you sit you're gonna remember the moves that made you feel like that."

"Yay me," she goaded and laughed softly into my neck before sinking her teeth into the flesh between my shoulder and neck. My dick twitched and grew thicker. Chloe's move of raw carnal need reminded me of how good we were together and I couldn't wait to be inside her. She was definitely my match in the sack and sometimes I only had to look at her across a crowded room and I felt my dick grow so hard I feared it would burst.

I'd never been happy in my heart until I knew her. Never been truly content until I made her mine, and I was determined to make sure I handled my daughter with the same respect I offered to Chloe, but I'd never allow her to come between us.

That afternoon when I knelt back on my heels between Chloe's legs, I took my time to peruse the beautiful curves of her body. The swell of her pert full breasts and her even satin skin mesmerized me. My eyes settled on hers— the incredible feature of hers that drew me to her so readily from the moment I saw them. A lump grew in my throat for all I felt for her.

Every time I was in this position I loved glancing down the valley between her breasts toward the curve of flesh right over her pussy and every time I did, my dick grew tighter in its skin. No one did it for me like her. No woman ever came close to how we connected. Whenever I saw her lying waiting in anticipation of what was to come the flat of her stomach palpated from the rapid beating of her heart. Knowing her body responded to my touch moved me.

Grasping her just above the knee my hand slid teasingly up the silky skin on her inner thigh and kept right on going. Delving into her folds the warm nectar was an open invitation to get up inside her and an instant dew drop dripped from my tip in excitement at the prospect. Sliding one digit into the tight space I felt her pussy pulsate around it, clamping tightly and holding me firmly inside. As soon as I felt her muscles clamp around my bony knuckle it ramped up my impatience to fill her deep.

Adjusting my position between her legs I gripping tightly at each hip watching my nails blanch under the pressure I exerted on her soft perfect flesh. My possessiveness tightened my chest as I yanked her butt up onto my thighs and skimmed the head of my dick lazily down her crease.

Seeing her eyelids droop at the sensation I stopped, smiled because I knew exactly what she wanted and teased my dick at the lips of her entrance. Chloe's eyes darkened, her need for more increasing as she wiggled her ass closer. I clamped my hands on her thighs and held her still, knowing it was driving her crazy.

"You want me?"

"I do."

"Tell me what you want, Chloe. I want to hear the words," I coaxed.

"Inside...I need you inside me," she answered.

"You need to be clearer than that. What do you want? You want me to fuck you, make love? Hard and fast, slow and sweet? What's it to be, darlin'?"

"Fuck me. Own me."

For the following three hours I worshiped her body, not with love, but with pure passion and my heartfelt desire from being inside her. Collapsing beside her drenched in sweat, I turned her face toward mine and kissed her slowly.

Even after we felt sated and heaved breathless I still found myself checking out that line of her body between her breasts and down to her belly button. I was still fully immersed in her beauty and fascinated by the sweaty sheen of her skin and the strong pulse that visibly beat in the vein on her neck. My hand skimmed over the flat of her stomach as I relished in the slightly damp feel of it and felt satisfied knowing I'd had that effect on her.

"Chloe Barclay, I love you more than life itself...never doubt that. You. Are. Mine." I reconfirmed in the event she had any shred of doubt left. Lying with our bodies entangled I stayed inside her as long as was possible then when we were no longer joined I turned her away from me and pulled her back close to my chest.

Inhaling deeply I let her amazing scent fill my lungs and cupped her breast in my hand. Feeling her heart still racing against her chest from what we'd done filled me with a sense of satisfaction. As I closed my eyes and felt myself drifting off to sleep her chest expanded then relaxed with a long sigh and smiled contented knowing she was happy each time I laid claim to her.

Chapter Nine

CYNICAL

Chloe

When Friday morning came nerves fluttered in my stomach and started to feed all the self-doubts I had managed to face since I became Gibson's wife. Most women would have killed to be in the position I was in, but after losing all confidence it was a slow process to regain it.

No matter how great I was at telling myself I deserved to be with my husband, there were still those rare occasions when it didn't take much to question my right to stay there. Facing Melody's mother was one of those days. I wasn't weak— far from it. But keeping the past suppressed sometimes felt more difficult than others.

Four days had passed since Gibson had told me about Melody and although I'd been given a little time to absorb the news I was nowhere near resigned to the fact our world had changed forever. There was no way I would allow my insecurities to rob Gibson of his gift so I knew I had to push past all of my feelings to support him and his, especially since his child was staying with us for the following four days.

Most of my anxieties weren't around her, but the woman who gave birth to her. As straightforward as Gibson was, unlike him I always looked beyond the fringes. After the way I was treated by my previous partner I felt cynical as to the motives behind the actions and decisions people made. *Why after six and a half years would you show up on someone's doorstep with something this big? What does it mean for Gibson, his daughter, her mother, and me?*

Gibson had arranged for a sympathetic reporter to handle the news because he knew it was better to give the disclosure and have some control than allow the paparazzi to trample all over the issue. Milo Serani was a reporter Gibson given a few exclusives to in the past and he told me he trusted Milo more than the others. The story was about to break and Gibson had ensured that Melody was in his care while this happened.

For the previous few days I'd watched Gibson closely and I could see his restlessness, so I wasn't surprised when he suddenly burst out the door and ran down the hill from the house. His powerful form pounded into the hard dirt as he took off at speed and became smaller and smaller until he disappeared out of sight. Then I knew the pressure was piling up on him.

Gibson was diagnosed with ADHD as a child and always took flight when he felt the pressure build in his head. He wasn't running from the situation, it was his way of controlling how his body functioned. It didn't worry me when he did it and I knew he'd be back, it was just a way of making sure he acted appropriately in the presence of his daughter. In a strange way I found it comforting to know I wasn't the only one with feelings of apprehension.

Piper came out the screen door onto the porch. I was sitting on a small stone bench with my feet on the wooden rails. Sliding a hand around my shoulders she gave me a forced grin.

"Do you feel worried, Chloe?" I glanced up at her and shielded my eyes from the sun.

"I'd be a fool if I said no," I answered honestly.

"I've only been here in the house a few days and I can see from how Gibson is with you he loves you very much, but this has to be a strain on your relationship." I studied her innocent face and realized Piper was much older than her years for all she'd endured, and nodded.

"We're trying not to let it come between us."

"You're a strong person, Chloe, and Gibson...well he dotes on you. I think he'll figure it out for all of you. He's not the man I've watched on T.V. while growing up. The man behind the rock star is much more awesome than the crude rock star his image portrays."

"Glad I'm not the only one who thinks that," I answered smiling because she'd seen his true worth. "I've never met anyone like him. Yet, when I first met him he's the last man on earth I'd have thought I'd marry."

"Well from what I've seen so far you're a match made in heaven. Ying and Yang my mom would have said. You pull each other straight. One can't fall because you are tethered to each other."

Tears sprang to my eyes at her description because it was similar to my own thoughts way back to something Gibson once said. From how he explained it I was the magnet and he was the shiny metal. Something about me drew him toward me and he stuck. He taught me that magnets attract and repel because they have lines of force that enter their south pole and exit the north. Opposite poles attract each other while similar ones repel. No doubt about it Gibson and I were opposites or just like Piper had said, ying and yang.

"I never meant to upset you," she said with a horrified look on her face. Before I could reply I heard the familiar engines in the distance alerting me to Jonny's arrival. I glanced at the sky and silently followed its descent with my eyes until the jet disappeared from view. At the same time I caught sight of Gibson on the ground, heading back toward the house.

"You didn't, Piper. What you've said was the perfect reminder I needed today as to why we'll make it through this." I turned and hugged her then held her away from me, "Glad you are here to support me in this. You're family now and we're all in this together." Piper smiled and glanced to the side. My eyes followed her just as Gibson reached the bottom of the steps and Piper hastily retreated to give us some privacy.

Breathless and sweaty he glanced up with a wide smile, closing one eye against the sun's glare. "I better get showered before showtime, darlin'. I've texted Jonny and figure if he does what I tell him we've got time for a quickie, want to join me?" He winked without a hint of nerves about him and nodded in the direction of our bedroom.

I smiled and laughed softly, "As much as I'm tempted I think I'll just hang here and be the welcoming party in the event you're too slow." Gibson grabbed me rubbing his sweaty face all over mine. I yelped in protest and he chuckled and grabbed my ass pulling me closer against his whole body "I'm marking you, Mrs. Barclay, if you won't let me come inside you this is the best I can do."

Releasing me from his grasp I swatted him playfully and he opened the screen door, "I'll be down in five, want to time me?" he asked in another teasing comment and I laughed. I knew he was trying to help me relax and by being attentive and caring for my feelings—he did.

No sooner did Gibson go inside when Piper came back out. She carried a pitcher of homemade Lemonade, glasses, and a bowl of fruit. Placing them on the patio table she swiftly went back inside and brought some salad forks and small frosted side plates.

"Forgive me for doing this, Chloe but I figured if we're sitting drinking and eating we'll have the upper hand. They are the ones coming into *your* home, so maybe you should own it? It is they who have to fit in after all...not us." She held her breath for my reply with a concerned look on her face.

"True. You're a mini-genius," I said and moved to a chair by the patio table. Piper poured us drinks and placed a couple of pieces of fruit on a small plate in front of me.

"There. Bring it," she said like a boss and I smiled widely.

"By the way I love you already," I offered with a quick hug.

"I love you too—both of you." No sooner were the words out of her mouth than we heard the engine of the Mercedes 4X4 as it came up the driveway. Piper grabbed my hand and squeezed. "You're not hard to love, Chloe. Melody will see that," she said with conviction.

I turned my head and the car stopped alongside the porch in the driveway. Conflicting feelings as to whether to go to her or to let them come to me tugged at my conscience. I settled for doing what was right and not what I'd do for the upper hand and stood up gracefully from my chair. I spun on my heel an made my way downstairs in time for Jonny to open the door and although I'd seen her picture already, I wasn't prepared for the beautiful woman who accompanied Melody— her mother, Kiran.

My heart thumped wildly in my chest, each beat made my lungs crush tighter then I realized I wasn't drawing breath. Inhaling deeply, I felt my cheeks burn because she was immaculately dressed in a peach chiffon dress and kitten heels with short dark hair that was styled to perfection. I glanced down at Melody and her huge almond shaped light grey eyes stole another breath. They were just like my husband's.

Our heads turned to the sound of the screen door creaking. Gibson stepped out onto the porch larger than life and looking incredibly appealing…and for a moment I figured he was too appealing. For the first time in my life I wished he were less so. I knew I had to show Kiran I wasn't threatened by her presence so I crouched down and stared into Melody's familiar eyes.

"Hello, little miss, you must be the famous Melody I've been hearing so much about."

Melody's eyes flitted back and forth across my face with a puzzled look, "Who are you?" she asked in all innocence. It felt like a slap in the face. Had no one spoken about me? *Does she not know I'm her dad's wife?* Was I going to be disappointment about me now she had a Mommy and a Daddy?

"This is Chloe my gorgeous wife. Remember I told you about her, Melody?"

"But she's not my mommy."

Gibson frowned and stepped forward. Crouching beside her he held her by her forearms and gave her a soft smile. "Nope, not your mommy but because she's my wife she's your step mommy. You're so special you get to have two mommies." Gibson placed his hand on her head and smoothed her hair before he straightened to his full height and towered above her.

"Now, you must be thirsty after your journey and I see that Chloe has some of that amazing lemonade she makes. Want to get some with me?" Melody turned and looked behind her to Kiran who stood quietly clutching her Armani purse and then the child turned back to look at me.

"Is that okay?" Her head turned from me to her mom again and I could see how confused she was as to who would give her permission.

"Kiran is it okay for Melody to have some fruit and lemonade?" I asked giving her, her rightful place.

"Not too much. She won't eat her lunch otherwise," Kiran warned.

"Alright, Mommy, don't get heavy with me, I'll only have half a glassful," she said rolling her eyes dramatically at Gibson. Kiran was behind her so couldn't see her face. I wanted to laugh and looked at Gibson who bit back a grin and tipped his chin into his chest to hide how funny he found her reply.

Clearing his throat he put one hand in his pocket and stuck the other in her direction. "Let's go before she changes her mind," he said nudging her arm with his hand. There was no hesitation in Melody and she shoved her small hand forward into his.

Gibson looked down at it and I could see how tiny it looked in his huge palm. Immediately his head snapped up to look at me and I saw how shocked the impact of her touch was to him. Without speaking he swallowed roughly and began to walk with her onto the porch.

I watched them go for a second then turned to Kiran. "You must be tired after your journey. Should we leave them to get acquainted? I'll show you to your accommodation." I flashed her a genuine smile but it faltered when I saw a smug look in return.

"Sure," she replied and eyed me from head to toe before directing her gaze squarely at my eyes. There was a challenge in her attitude that I didn't miss. Dressed in jean shorts and a fitted tank top I'd felt my attire appropriate for meeting a child at my own home, but Kiran had made me feel considerably underdressed and dowdy in comparison to how she'd presented herself.

Despite how affected I was I'd never have shown it because I felt she'd dressed for my husband and not for the occasion, and I was determined not to allow her the satisfaction of knowing she'd affected me in any way.

Jonny gave me a slow smile, winked, grabbed Kiran bags then situated himself between us. His action served as a protective gesture which told me I hadn't read her wrong. When I led her down the path toward the back of the cabin and out toward the pool house she suddenly stopped.

"Wait, where exactly are you taking me?"

"Guest house," Jonny replied before I could speak.

"We're not good enough to stay in the main house with the rest of you?" she asked with an indignant tone to her voice.

"Tsk, Gibson should have explained. Our house only has six bedrooms, Jonny and Jerry, Gibson's security, Emma, who's mine, Piper, then Gibson and I. Which means there is only one spare. It only has one twin bed in it as we've never used it so there's not enough room for the two people. You need to remember, Kiran we weren't expecting you."

Jonny gave a wry smile at my reply and continued to look straight ahead. He saw she looked dumbfounded.

"I'm sure the accommodation in the pool house will prove very comfortable, Kiran. There are two king rooms and one queen in there as well as a sitting room, kitchen, and two bathrooms. As the main house and pool house are built on two levels you'll find a porch at the back with a hottub and sauna. The view of the mountains is actually prettier from there than the one from here at the main house."

"But the pool?"

Jonny piped up, "Don't worry the cover on the pool is extremely taut. I can walk on it so it's perfectly safe for Melody. As soon as Gibson and Chloe knew she existed Chloe ordered this to make sure she could never fall into the water. I can assure you they both take Melody's safety very seriously. Then there is Emma, Jerry, and I, someone patrols twenty-four seven as well as the CCTV guys."

Kiran shook her head like she was displeased at being fobbed off and the way she had spoken to me only served to say I was right about my initial assessment of her. "I need my baby to be safe. No one knows her like I know her—"

"Absolutely, hence the extra precautions we've taken," Jonny replied again. I was thankful for his interjections but I knew I had to be forthright in my arguments otherwise I'd give Kiran the impression I was weak.

I broke free of the line we were walking in and stepped forward with the key, "If you don't want to stay here, of course neither Gibson, nor I would force the matter. If you'd prefer we can book you into a hotel in town it would just mean Melody traveling twenty minutes in a car twice a day while you are here."

Panic registered and I saw she wasn't expecting me to ship her off somewhere else. I found her behavior very telling considering Gibson's sob story of there being three generations in one tiny apartment and his daughter and Kiran sharing a bed. Jonny wandered around opening the plantation shutters and shards of light filled the cream and lime décor of the sitting room.

An eight piece sectional sofa in cream curved around an oval coffee table and faced the huge television. Gibson and the boys loved watching football in the pool house while us wives and girlfriends lounged out by the pool.

"The bedrooms are down here," I said but didn't wait for her to follow me. Pushing one then another door open I showed her how light and airy they were and how opulent the décor was. Most people would give their eye teeth to have a home built to the standard and designed perfectly to accommodate guests like ours was.

"I suppose Gibson can always come here to discuss arrangements and support for our daughter," she offered in what I could only assume was another jibe at my position.

"I'll definitely mention your comments when we go back. Are you staying here to unpack or are you coming back up to the house?" Jonny wandered toward the door and held it open on cue. "I'll freshen up then come back over. Can you leave him here until I'm ready to come back?" she asked nodding at Jonny.

"Sorry Kiran, now that I'm home I'm on duty again for these guys. Where Chloe goes I go...or Jerry, or Emma. You'll be fine just follow the path back and we'll be on the porch."

Chapter Ten

HURT

Gibson

WHEN I HEARD CHLOE AND JONNY'S CONVERSATION I KNEW KIRAN was still at the pool house.

"Fuck. Meeow, she's a handful. All the way here she kept pushing the flight attendant for information about you and Gibson."

My ears pricked up because there had obviously been some kind of a fracas once Kiran was out of my sight. I didn't think for one minute that it would have been Chloe who instigated it but I wasn't sure how she'd have responded. Feelings were tentative at best with this delicate situation.

"You saw her at the gig, right? How did she behave then?" Chloe asked.

"Good as gold. Nothing like I've seen today. Sweet, humble, didn't want anything from anyone and seemed as if she just wanted Melody to know her father. Completely different to just now she barely hid her bitch side there and she's only just arrived. I'd question Melody was Gibson's if the poor kid didn't look so fucking eerily alike his mom from that picture."

My blood immediately warmed from Jonny's response. Maybe she underestimated me. Just because I was civil and accommodating didn't mean I was going to let her fuck with the life I have with Chloe.

"Wish I felt strong enough for this," Chloe mumbled and my heart squeezed tight because I'd hurt her.

"What the fuck, girl. Remember how far you've come you can be a real badass when your turf is threatened. Don't let her push you into a corner," Jonny responded. I could have kissed him for his honesty. It was exactly what Chloe needed to hear.

"I won't. I just don't want her holding Melody over Gibson's head if she doesn't get her way." My nostrils flared as my temper was rose further. No matter who Kiran was to my daughter I would never allow her to be anything but cordial toward my wife. I'd go to court for my rights to see Melody if necessary.

"You forget who my boss is. That Dude has the ability to make her go away should that be necessary."

Chloe's voice came back sharply, "No. Don't even joke about that. I'd never take a child away from its mother no matter how much it helped our situation or how much I wanted a kid of my own. I'll deal with her don't you worry I just don't have the stomach to do anything that would affect Gibson and his relationship with her while it's still at a fledgling stage."

My chest swelled with frustration and love in equal measure that Chloe had to be impacted so much and I wondered if I'd done the right thing bringing Melody to our home so soon. Jonny was patting her back as they came into view, he spoke softer but I still heard what he said.

"Remember I got you, so does Gibson. You need to get the fuck away from her just scratch your nose. I'll give you an out." Chloe chucked at his cloak and dagger signal code and glanced up to look for me. Her breath caught in her throat and I realized she saw Melody sitting on my knee. Tears welled in her eyes and I fought past the lump that grew rapidly in my throat when I saw how affected she was.

"Hey, and here's my other pretty girl. Did you find everything you needed?" I asked, reaching out for her. Lifting Melody from my knee I sat her in the seat next to me. As always whenever I saw Chloe it was never enough. I had to touch her. Taking my hand she stepped forward. I opened my legs and she walked into them. Swiftly I gripped her hip, pulled her down onto my lap, and hugged her tightly.

"Daddy sat me on his knee too," Melody said with a beaming smile. Chloe leaned back to look at her and smiled.

"Really? Then... wow you're extra special because he only usually wants me to sit here," she replied with an upward inflection in her voice like she was surprised.

Melody looked pleased with Chloe's response. "I didn't know I was going to get a daddy and *another* mommy when I went to the concert. What do I call you, Mommy or Chloe?"

My first reaction was to tell her to call her what felt the most normal to her but then I considered Kiran's feelings and said we should ask her mom about that. Personally, I wanted her to call Chloe her mom.

"But if you belong to me and not her shouldn't I get to say so?" She had a point and I loved how she had said in such a natural way that Chloe belonged to her. Difficult decisions always had the simplest solutions to kids.

"What are we talking about?" Kiran's voice sounded light and out of keeping with Chloe and Jonny's conversation about her. It put me on my guard.

"I don't know what I'm to call Chloe. If she's my other mom then do I call h—" Kiran shut her down.

"That's what you call her. Chloe. She's not your mom, I am. I don't want you to get confused about who has responsibility for you," she snapped.

"But she's my ... what did you call people attached to others?" I frowned for a minute and looked at Kiran wondering what Melody was talking about.

"Relatives, but she's not—" Kiran looked at me as if she forgot herself for a moment and I was given an insight to her real feelings about Chloe.

"I mean, Chloe is married to your dad, but you're little so I don't think we should be confusing you further by asking you to call both of us Mommy."

"I'm not confused. You're my Tummy Mummy. I know that."

I couldn't hold back the expression I wore. Melody wasn't exactly a rocker's name but damn she was every bit as badass as a rock star's daughter should be.

"Whatever you want to call me is cool by me, but maybe we should start by you calling me Chloe for now. I mean Mom has such a special status. I think it's a name reserved for the person who's been there for you since you were little, Chloe is okay with me."

I glanced at my wife who was the voice of reason and who had given Kiran her place with her child. It reminded me once again of how much I loved her and why.

With the name issue resolved Chloe gestured at the pitcher of Lemonade. "Would you like a cold drink, lunch will be ready in," she checked her wristwatch, "fifteen minutes." Kiran sat on the other side of me while my arm tightened around Chloe's waist.

Piper came out of the screen door and picked up the pitcher before Chloe could reach for it. It was as if she were standing on the other side of the door while the name conversation had taken place. She poured Kiran a glass of Lemonade and then one for herself, and sat down on the other side of Melody. I glanced at her and realized I hadn't introduced anyone.

"Oh, sorry, this is Piper—"

"His other daughter," she said without making eye contact with anyone. Leaning forward she picked some fruit from the bowl on the table and placed it on a small plate.

"I didn't know you already had a kid," Kiran blurted in a voice filled with alarm. Immediately I saw her ego deflate, as if her status, had been diluted by what Piper had disclosed.

"Well you know now," Piper said flatly and turned to Melody. So I guess that makes us half-sisters." Watching Piper I saw a side of her I hadn't seen before. She was a strong young woman and she was being a fierce ally to Chloe.

"So who is your mom?"

Piper glanced at me then to Chloe. "Chloe. She's my mom."

"So you call her Mom?"

"No, I call her Chloe and I call my dad, Gibson. Chloe isn't my tummy mom either. My Mom has gone to Heaven so Chloe and Gibson take care of me now."

"Did they pick you like that man in the movie, 'Annie'?"

"No." Piper chuckled. "My Tummy Mom was already living here with me. After she had to go to be an angel in Heaven Gibson and Chloe became my parents."

"Wow you were lucky you didn't have to go to an Ostrich."

I burst out laughing and Piper giggled at Melody's mistake.

"I was extremely lucky. You're lucky too, Melody. My mom and dad are fabulous people."

Kiran wriggled uncomfortably in her chair clearly put out by Piper's presence. I could see she figured it made her my relationship with Melody less of a big deal because Chloe and I had another young person to occupy our time. Of course, that wasn't the case, and it wasn't the time for games. Melody was my flesh and blood and I was damned if I would allow her security to become a pissing contest.

Chloe pushed off me to stand and my hand slid free of her. "I'm going to check on lunch, Piper can you come and help please?" Jonny had already gone off to find Emma no doubt filling her in on the deal with Kiran and ensuring she had Chloe's back.

"Can I come as well? Mom can I go with them?" Kiran looked first to Melody then to me. I saw the instant Kiran knew she had an opportunity to have me on my own.

"Sure. Stay back from the kitchen stove remember," she told her as we watched her hurry inside after the others.

Seconds after she was out of sight she turned and stared at me. "I never thought I'd be sitting on Gibson Barclay's porch drinking Lemonade," she said putting her glass to her mouth and taking a long draw of it. "Very refreshing," she added before placing her lipstick stained glass on the patio table.

"I want joint custody. Not sure how to make it work but that's what I want." There was no point in anything but talking straight.

"Her life is with me in Chicago, Gibson. She wanted to meet you, unless you move to Chicago that's impossible. Her schooling and life are there."

"She can be home schooled and have social clubs in both places. Her tutors can tell us what she needs to do ahead of time and we'll ensure she never feels misplaced. She'll have two lots of friends and twice the activities but just on the same days as she would at home. That way her routines will feel regulated. She's young, she'll adapt."

Kiran's face paled and she sat staring open mouthed.

"The alternative is you move here...to Colorado," I stated.

"And what? Live in your pool house? I'm sure Chloe would adore having the threat of me around."

"You're no threat to my wife—let's be straight about that from the get-go."

"No? You're naïve if you believe that. We have a child together, Gibson. She can't compete with that. We're connected for the rest of our lives. Joined together by our beautiful daughter."

"True, we have a daughter together, but my relationship is with her. Not with you. I'm willing to fund an appropriate place for you all to live. A place where she has a secure yard to bring friends, a nice home with her own bedroom and I'll give her everything she needs, Kiran. I'd be doing it to support her, not you. If it brings your standard of living up then that's a bonus, but my motivation is Melody. You are the mother of my child and I respect that part of the relationship, but I won't let you fuck with my life or my wife, you got me?"

Kiran looked to her nails then back to my face. "Does Chloe know how we met?"

"No. We've never discussed it. Why would I? I don't want to hurt you but I was smashed-off-my- face drunk the night we made Melody. It's a wonder I could even get it up, let alone fuck someone. The condom must have split because I wasn't taking enough care. If I'm honest in my mind most of the night is blank." Standing up I maneuvred around the table.

"Lunch will be about done, think about what I said, one way or another I'm taking an equal role in her upbringing. As soon as you knew she was mine you should have told me. I've missed six and a half years of her life and now that you've told her about me, the last thing I'm gonna let happen is for her to think I only want her on special occasions."

"It's my decision where and how I bring her up, Gibson. All I wanted was for you to know she was out there and provide us with a little support."

"And you think coming to my home and insulting my wife is the best way to achieve that? I see how you're dressed and frankly, you're still trying to be the same tease you were back in that nightclub. I don't know what you thought was going to happen when you brought me into the frame at this late stage but I guess you've realized I'm not a guy who excuses his actions. I've never made excuses for the decisions I've made but I always accept responsibility for them."

Leaving her, I stood next to the table, pulled open the screen door, and never looked back. Stepping over the threshold I saw Chloe standing on the opposite side of the room. Her eyes were trained on me and I knew instantly she'd heard most of the conversation I'd had. I hadn't exactly been quiet when I had put my points across.

Taking a deep breath to calm my jets I strode over and pulled her in for a hug. Immediately, Melody ran over and hugged my leg as well. I was surprised at how quickly she became attached to me. "What's that fabulous smell?" I asked by way of a diversion.

"Macaroni cheese. My favorite." I already knew that because I'd asked Kiran that on the phone. It pleased me to know this because it was also one of mine.

"Yum, let's wash our hands and grab a chair before it's all gone," I teased walking toward the bathroom. Even though she'd never been in my home before Melody followed like it was the most natural thing in the world. Her confidence and open mind captured my heart and I marvelled at how easily she adapted to her new situation.

Although it was early days I felt in my bones the risk of sharing custody was worth it. Life with her mom would be half a life and I had a right to make sure I didn't allow her to settle for that.

Chapter Eleven

NOT ANAL

Chloe

Strange that I had been so determined not to be privy to the conversation between Gibson and Kiran yet I along with everyone else in the kitchen had heard almost every word they had said. If Melody had understood what was said she didn't appear to be interested in the raised voices of Gibson and her mother.

Piper shot me a look when Gibson went into the bathroom followed by Melody and asked in a low voice, "Are you okay?" I nodded and went back to what I was doing, placing the food on the ovenproof mats on the table.

The screen door creaked and Kiran came inside. She stood in on the other side of the door and looked much less sure of herself than she had when I took her to the pool house. Glancing over at her I knew instantly by the way she hugged her upper arms her cocky confident attitude from earlier had been dented by her intimate chat with Gibson. Her eyes scanned the room no doubt looking for Melody so I helped her out.

"Melody has gone to wash her hands for lunch. There's a bathroom down the hall if you want to freshen up."

"No thanks, I just did that before I came back up here," she said like she wanted nothing to do with me.

"You can take a seat, we're about finished here," Piper told her gesturing with her head to the dining table chairs.

"Anywhere in particular?"

"No we're not anal here, we don't have set chairs." I smiled because I knew she'd made that up on the spot, she'd only had a few meals with us and each time we'd all sat in the same seats. I knew Piper was walking a line. We weren't friends— I was supposed to be her guardian, but she was proving her loyalty toward us so I saw no harm in what she said so long as she wasn't outright rude.

Gibson came back down the hall with Melody hanging upside down from his shoulder, "I'm not sure if we should let this one eat, she has a mouth full of sass already," he informed us then swung her upright and set her down on the floor.

"Where are you sitting?" she asked Gibson with her hands on her hips but a look of adoration in her eyes.

"Depends. Where are you sitting?"

"On a chair?"

"See what I mean?" he asked all of us and grabbed her by her waist then began tickling her.

"I'm s ... sorry," she blurted through her sweet- sounding giggles as Gibson made her breathless with his hands.

"Alright that's enough," Kiran said breaking into their moment of joy together. After six and a half years I felt Gibson was entitled to play with his little girl. I shot her a look and I'm sure it conveyed my sentiments of wanting to throat punch her for breaking the moment, but she didn't bat an eyelid. Instead she picked up her napkin, shook it out and laid it across her lap.

"Sit, Melody. Remember your manners at the table and that we are guests in someone's home."

"It's her home too now," Gibson almost spat.

I hated Kiran for becoming authoritarian but I felt a little empathy for her plight. Since Melody had been born she'd had her all herself. From my observations I could see she already regretted her decision to share her with Gibson and his extended family.

———

Somehow, we all made it through lunch without throwing a punch or killing each other before Gibson addressed Melody's mom and asked if he could show Melody around his soundproof music room. He loved his mini recording suite. It was his sanctuary and he'd spend hours in there making rough drafts of his music scores and new songs before sharing them with the world. Melody jumped down from the table and tugged at her mom's dress begging for permission.

Before Kiran could answer Melody turned with her hands clasped tight with excitement and asked Gibson if he had a microphone. When Gibson nodded with a grin on his face she asked if she could sing for him. Piper stood and shoved the sleeves of her cardigan up her arms in an awkward gesture.

Can I come too?" she asked. For the first time that day she showed her uncertainty as to what she was to us.

"Sure, sweetheart. Wait until you hear Piper sing," he told Melody. Piper couldn't contain how good he'd made her feel and looked like she was melting when she looked back at him.

Melody looked excitedly at Piper and grinned again. "Gosh you really *are* like Annie from the movie you're an Ostrich *and* you can sing." Once again no one corrected her on the choice of word and Gibson smiled widely at Piper.

"Guess as you're an Ostrich and I'm your dad as well as Melody's you'd better head back there with us," he told her nodding in the direction of the music suite and chuckled.

Dropping her napkin onto the table Piper turned to face me. "Please may I leave the table, Chloe?" A small smile played on her lips.

"Sure. Have fun," I offered, then stood and began to gather the pasta bowls together. Kiran placed her fork in her bowl and sat back wiping her mouth. I could see her mind ticking over and for the first time I almost understood the term Gibson used with me when he told me he could hear what I was thinking. I could imagine the conversation going on in her head about me and none of it was particularly flattering.

Out of the side of my eye I saw Emma sitting on the sofa in the spot in the great room nearest to the kitchen and knew immediately Jonny had brought her up to speed. I wasn't afraid to be alone with

Kiran but I was glad someone was there to bear witness should she start dishing out shit that I had to defend.

When Kiran thought it was safe to speak she stood and began to help clear the dishes. "It's really weird seeing Gibson with Melody." I thought it was a genuine comment and nodded because it felt strange for me, and figured it must have been totally weird to have your daughter meet her dad when it had only been two of them for so long.

"I bet," was all I offered and continued to clear up.

"Odd and embarrassing for you too, I imagine."

"I'm not embarrassed my husband has a daughter. In the past I had figured it strange there weren't more Melody-like spawn running around."

"I didn't mean that I meant coming face-to-face with someone he had sex with. I mean I've been where you are now." Fury rushed through every fiber of my body.

"No. Kiran you're mistaken. You were a quick fuck for Gibson. He used women for sport. Gibson loves me. He never loved any of the others. I'm sorry but I am not allowing you to compare what you were to him to what he has with me."

"Well he never got time to love me, but I can tell you now he loved what he did to me. And he's been the best partner I've ever had. He ruined me. Doesn't it scare you even just a little bit that he may want another taste of me?"

My eyes darted to Emma who had rounded the sofa and was stood resting her ass against the back of it just out of sight. I could see her but Kiran had no idea she was there.

"Don't think I didn't hear the conversation you just had out there. Gibson was drunk when he screwed you. I heard him say it. You were just another one and done in a nightclub before we met."

"I wasn't a fuck against some alleyway outside a nightclub, Chloe. He came to the gentlemen's club I worked at. I gave him a lap dance and we took it from there. The way he took me was so controlling and demanding you can't tell me he wouldn't remember it."

"Holy shit, that was...you?" I mumbled in disbelief as shock made my eyes practically bug out of my head. Not only was Gibson there when Melody was conceived in a sick way so was I. When I realized who she was my mind flashed back to an incident when I lived in New York.

During that night my cell ringing had woken me up. Gibson and I weren't together at that point but his cell phone accidently called mine. A little disorientated from being in bed I listened for a few minutes then realized I was listening to two people having sex.

"What was me? Did he tell you about me?" she asked looking for some recognition she had meant something.

"No he never mentioned you. I know all about it though. Let me see what I remember... *"Oh, sweet Jesus, YES! Right there ... right there, don't stop ... harder,"* What else did I hear? *"Damn! That feels sooo fucking good, baby. You're very good at this, honey I love your big dick.* Am I ringing any bells?" Inside my heart was breaking in two because I was staring at the face of a woman my husband had fucked. I'd seen him do it to other women before and there were some things I could never unsee, but to hear it in my own bedroom and know he made a child with her was much worse. To know the one incident that haunted me most had resulted in a child was devastating.

My chest felt crushingly tight and I hurt all over but I knew I could never allow her to know how much her revelation had cut me in two.

"You see, Kiran, Gibson and I weren't together when he 'did you'. And believe me that's how Gibson described the many hundreds if not thousands of women he fucked while he was trying to find me.

You weren't the first I'd heard make those declarations about the effect he had on them either. You see Gibson and I go way back. Off the top of my head I could name at least two dozen girls he fucked back then that I personally saw him do it to. So despite everything you think you are know this... Gibson is *mine*. He'll always be mine."

Emma strolled into the room and leaned against the wall. "Hey, Chloe, everything okay?" she asked innocently.

"Yep we're fine here, thanks. Give us five please, would you?" Emma glanced at Kiran then back to me like she wasn't sure she should leave me and I offered a smile of reassurance. I wondered who she thought she needed to protect because my feelings toward Kiran weren't the most loving. However, it was my opportunity to set things straight with Kiran because she had to learn from the beginning how formidable I could be if she pissed in my yard.

All the while Emma and I were talking I knew Kiran was mulling over her options and unless I'd read her wrongly I knew she'd be mustering ammunition to fire back. Emma moved over to the entrance of the great room again and retook her position from earlier. Once again, Kiran had no idea she was monitoring the situation between us.

"Have you any idea how hard it has been to take care of everyone this past six years?"

"If you'd told Gibson about Melody neither of you would have wanted for anything."

"How could I tell him when he had you? I thought he'd grow tired—"

"And what? You'd swoop in with his daughter and console him? You have no idea of the kind of man you are dealing with. You underestimated him and you've underestimated the love we have for each other. Not that it's any of your business but the shit we've dealt is much bigger than discovering Gibson has a love child."

"She's not coming here to live."

"That's your choice, however, as someone with Melody's best interests at heart I'd politely warn you not to take Gibson on by using the child you have together. The person you'll hurt most is Melody. She's not going to be a child forever and one day she'll be able to make her own choice of where she wants to be. Don't be the bitter parent, you'll push her away. You know how charismatic Gibson is. How likely is she to choose you when she has someone as beguiling as him? That isn't a threat, Kiran, you must know how irresistible he is."

"I wish I'd never taken her to that concert."

"Well I'm glad that you did. For once I think you did the right thing, even if it was a little late in the day. Again, I'd remind you she won't be a child forever. I'd hate her to resent you for not giving her the opportunity to see what a fantastic Dad she has."

Kiran thought in silence and the air between us grew heavy.

"I'm not asking you to like me. To be frank, I don't know how I'd feel if the situation were reversed and I know how it feels from my side of the fence but I do want to say this. Melody...she's a real credit to you. You should be proud of all you've achieved with her. She's a beautiful ray of sunshine and I can see Gibson has already fallen hard for her."

I could see my Kiran's face she wasn't expecting my praise.

"Thank you for keeping her and not taking the easy way out. I can't imagine how difficult life must have been for you at times. You've taken the first steps to offering a better life for Melody by allowing Gibson in."

"It's up to the three of us how we move forward," Kiran offered in a firm tone. I stared at her for a moment puzzled then I understood she didn't see a role for me with Melody, but before I could respond Gibson set her straight on that.

"Four. It's up to the four of us...five if you count Piper. We're all family in one way or another, but Chloe's always level headed when needs to be said." He walked over toward me and slipped his hand around my waist asserting his possessive and protective side. "I've left our girls singing a duet down in the suite. Piper looks a bit miffed that Melody has coaxed her into singing songs from that musical she keeps going on about." No matter what else was happening both Kiran and I couldn't help smiling at his comment.

"She's too damned cute to argue with," he said on a chuckled and shook his head. "I thought my troubles with women were over when I met you," Gibson said, cradling my head affectionately and kissed the tip of my nose. Turning to address Kiran he said, "I only heard the tail end of what Chloe was saying, but from what I heard she was talking a lot of sense. She usually does."

"Then I need to move to Colorado. How does that work?" she asked in a clipped tone.

Gibson grinned and his hand slipped down to my butt. He squeezed it tightly and turned his intense gaze on me, "How do you feel about that, darlin'?" he asked, seeking my approval.

The last thing I wanted was regular contact with Kiran but I figured it was better to manage her than not have any input and complain later if the arrangements didn't feel right.

"I think it's the most sensible solution. I'm sure Gibson will do what he can to make the transition as smooth as possible and unless you are both at loggerheads I'm almost convinced you'll work out a plan for custody that suits everyone. There are times when Gibson's not here due to work commitments but his load is lighter these days now we've learned to balance the band's commitments and home life."

Kiran looked a little uncertain, like she hadn't expected any of what was happening. I figured she was thinking it wasn't exactly what she wanted at all but knew it was the best deal for Melody. "There's my mom..."

"No problem. I'll set up a call with a local realtor through Jonny and we'll have you meet with them in town. No one comes here to the house apart from the band and no one knows this place is mine. I suggest you continue to respect that, Kiran. There's a lot of crazies that go with my work. This way ensures our daughter and my family are always safe."

Chapter Twelve

WAITING FOR SUPERMAN

Gibson

IT WASN'T UNTIL MELODY AND KIRAN WERE SITUATED IN THE POOL house for the night that I finally relaxed. Tension gripped my body for most of the day and I was glad I ran before they arrived. I'd have found it hard to keep my cool with Melody's mother otherwise.

When she met me in Chicago at that gig she had been so convincing that I'd taken her to be a sweet girl who'd made a mistake out of desperation when she got with me. The woman who arrived with my child today was nothing like her at all. Kiran had shown her true colors and I was thankful for Chloe's level nature. Any other woman would have had a knock-down-drag-out fight with her the way she kept goading Chloe. It was thanks to her I never lost it altogether with Kiran.

The craving I had for alcohol was stronger than ever but spirits and I didn't get on. Since I'd been with Chloe I had come to recognize alcohol was my nemesis. Alcoholic drinks always compounded stupid judgments I made.

I fought the urge and reached for the refrigerator door. Eying the apple juice I pulled out the clear container went to reach for a glass then stopped. Chloe had gone over to the refuge center with Emma so

I did the one thing that grossed her out and drunk half the contents straight from the plastic bottle.

Piper came downstairs with her earbuds in and I knew she was listening to herself from the recording I'd made of her earlier. She was a phenomenal singer and I had no doubts the moment Syd heard her she'd be given a deal. It wasn't just how good her range was it was the distinctive tone and the way she meshed the mix and made an individual arrangement for each song she sang. It appeared she could make any number her own.

After all she'd been through I was tempted to hand everything to her on a plate but she had a lot to learn. It was one thing to have talent but these days that wasn't enough. Stamina and the thirst to succeed were almost the key factors with the ability and network coming a close second.

"I hope that's one of my albums you're listening to," I said, playfully.

Pulling the earbuds out she furrowed her brow, "Sorry I didn't hear you, I was listening to "Waiting for Superman" by my favorite band, Daughtry," she replied and I decided I really loved this kid. Her sly smile indicated she'd heard exactly what I asked.

"Where's Chloe?"

I nodded at the window, "She's gone over the hill," we never referred to the retreat by name unless Chloe and I were alone.

"I wish she'd said she was going. I'd have gone with her."

"She had a new family arrive so she's gone to welcome them in. You did good today, by the way, I was proud of you." The gate buzzer sounded before I could continue. Emma had gone with Chloe and I was expecting Jerry because Jonny had the evening off. I held my finger up as if to say hold that thought and went to look at the CCTV. It wasn't Jerry but Simon the bass player from the band. I buzzed him in and Jerry followed in his car before the gates close again. I retook my seat in the great room.

Simon opened the door and Jerry waved and went upstairs.

"Yo, how's it hangin'?"

"Better now they've gone to bed," I replied referring to our visitors.

"It went well today?"

"Yeah, 'cept Kiran isn't exactly a shrinking violet."

"Damn. I guess she'll learn when you put her in her place at some point, Gib."

Piper had gone upstairs when the gate buzzer had sounded but came back down with a cardigan on. "I'm gonna take a short walk I feel pretty restless," she said.

Simon looked over at her and his tongue almost fell out. He watched her open and closed the door behind her. As soon as she'd gone I smacked him upside the head. "Lay a finger on her and you're gonna be dead meat."

"For fuck sake, what do you take me for? I was only looking, she's a kid."

"Exactly. Don't be a dick, you shouldn't be looking at all." Simon rubbed the back of his neck and looked awkward.

"I didn't mean to check her out. I was worrying about how you're gonna keep other guys out of that one's panties."

My tension about him lifted because I knew what he meant. I'd had the same thoughts myself and once I knew she really could sing, and had a real crack at the music industry it made me even more nervous. If Syd really did take her on it would be down to Chloe and my guidance to coach her and ensure no dirty bastard tricked her into bed for their personal pleasure.

From what I knew of Piper she was savvy and smart mouthed. When I saw how she dealt with Kiran and covered Chloe's back I figured she wasn't naïve. Chloe was around her age when I first saw her around. Not that I really knew her then.

"She sings," I said.

"Doesn't every teenage girl?"

"That was my first reaction when she told me she sang, but no— I mean she really has some serious pipes, Dude."

"You heard her in the shower?"

"I had her down in the music suite today with Melody. She can sing practically anything, Simon. No joke I felt goosebumps and the hair on my scalp stood on end. I'm gonna speak to Syd about her. It's what she wants to do with her life."

"Maybe she could come and do some backing tracks for us? A

female voice on a few of new numbers?"

"No way. This kid isn't a backing singer. She'll sell out stadiums if she gets the right support."

"Why don't you manage her?"

"Get the fuck out of here. When do you suppose I fit that in with everything else I got going on?"

Simon sighed, "Syd it is then. If she's as good as you think she is you'll need to get her some serious protection because there's a load of horny bastards hangin' around in our line of work."

My jaw ticked in anger as my teeth grated together. "No joke. If she is staying with us then she needs a detail of her own now anyway. I'll speak to Emma, Jerry, and Jonny, maybe set up some interviews. It's not gonna be long before she's out at parties and...fuck! I don't think I thought this parenting thing through enough," I said, grimacing with worry as I ran my hands through my hair.

Simon chuckled, "Well she's got four dads not one if she's yours. Len, Mick, and I will be sure to pick up the slack where we can."

Glancing over to him I figured they were probably the last people I'd leave her alone with. "I got this, y'all can keep your grubby paws to yourselves."

Simon held his hands innocently, "Whatever you say, Gibson. She's a kid. I'd never touch her."

"She's only a few months short of her eighteenth birthday, Simon. I know you like 'em young, so you can count this as your official warning. Touch her and I'll fucking end you."

"Jesus Christ, Gib. I'd never dream of—" The door opened and Chloe came inside followed by Piper. Chloe rubbed her upper arms with both hands.

"Brr, its chilly outside tonight. I noticed the temperature dropped a lot as soon as the sun went down. Hey, Simon."

The temperature inside was heated but I knew Simon had been warned and let the subject drop. I took myself off to the fridge, grabbing a couple of beers then gestured for him to follow me down to the music suite.

Once in the mini studio I played Simon one of the tunes I'd recorded with Piper that day. Wide eye he stopped mid-swig of his beer, "Fuck me, she's incredible. Who would have thought a voice like that would come out of a kid her size?" I knew what he meant Piper couldn't have weighed more than a hundred and ten pounds.

We listened to her a bit more then I played him the two new arrangements I'd written. Simon played around with the base until he had the perfect beat down for the numbers then he went home. By the time I went back to the great room no one was up. Climbing the stairs I walked quietly until I reached our bedroom.

When I opened the door I saw Chloe lying under the covers, the moon making streaks of light across the bed. Closing the door, I took myself into the bathroom and followed my night time routine then headed to bed. I slid between the sheets and sleepily Chloe automatically wrapped her naked, warm-as-toast body around mine. Her feet slid the length from my knee to toes then back before she coiled it around it like a snake round a tree branch. Her second aimed higher.

My arms wound around her waist and I pulled her to straddle my body then lay her on my chest. My hands slid down to cradle the globes of her ass. Not content with holding them I pressed her body hard against mine. She was an amazing woman, my wife and lying with her skin to skin was one of my favorite things in the world to do. It definitely came before standing before a stadium of seventy thousand.

"You were amazing today, darlin', I know Kiran was being a bitch and tried to push your buttons. You did well not to let her get you all riled up and took the higher ground. I loved your calmness, and seeing you failing to absorb her venom was a pleasure to watch. You made me so fucking proud, Chloe."

I traced my fingertips lazily over the skin on her back then placed it at the back of her head, pinning her cheek to my chest. We lay silent as I waited for Chloe to gather her thoughts.

"I didn't feel calm inside. You don't want to know what was going on in my head about what I wanted to do to her but it involved using a double-edged axe." She traced her finger over my pecs and repositioned her head over my heart.

My chest tightened at the words because Chloe would never hurt anyone so I knew it had been a horrible experience for her. It couldn't have been easy to sit and bite her tongue when her world was threatened in the way it was by my change in circumstance.

"You're such a badass, Chloe. Remind me not to get on the wrong side of you," I replied.

"It's gonna take a little adjusting and I know it's not ideal Kiran living in the same place but I'll make sure she's far enough away not to be a burden. I'm also gonna have Melody dropped and returned by Emma so that there's as little contact between the three adults as possible. Like I said, Chloe, she's the mother of my kid and I'll respect her for that but I'm not stupid enough to get into another dialogue with her once the arrangements are made."

I felt relieved that Gibson had the strength of character to put his foot down with Kiran.

"Charlotte can deal with any queries she has and I'll respond through her and when I've found her a property, that issue can be dealt with through the realtors and my lawyers can draw up a legal agreement."

Chloe lifted her head and looked up at me by the light of the moon. Her gorgeous eyes captured my attention and I stared into them. "That makes me happy. The last thing I want is for us adults to be at each other's throats while Melody is trying to flit back and forth between our homes."

"Thank you, darlin', I don't deserve you." My chest tightened again because although Chloe was being brave about our whole change in family dynamics they had to have impacted on her.

"Nonsense, Gibson. Look at the shit I dragged you into at the beginning of us. You didn't turn your back on me even in my darkest hour. You could have had any woman in the world lying here with you now, yet you rode the storm with me. We fix each other. It's just what we do. For what it's worth Melody is the most beautiful child I've ever seen. Even though you haven't influenced her she's you. I mean your personality runs through her. God knows what a handful she's going to be when she's a teenager."

Chloe grinned at my wide eyes because in all the time we'd been trying for a child our own in my mind they were never female. Girls were the stuff nightmares were made of. They had pimply teens with raging hormones lusting after them, spinning them lines just to dip their dicks. Whenever Chloe said she wanted a girl my blood used to run cold.

"I can hear you thinking, Gibson."

I snickered, "Ya think? I'm gonna get me the biggest, scariest shotgun a license can buy, and two Barettas; maybe a Glock or two..." I was joking but not really. Melody and Piper needed protecting from dirty fuckers like I had been in my youth. It made me feel bad for all the Moms and Dads who must have seen me arriving at their doors when I was a teen.

When Chloe began wiggling her pubic bone over my bare-naked dick it started to fill with the friction until it sprang to attention. "Oh, it's like that is it?" I teased in a sarcastic voice then flipped her over onto her back and got between her legs. Grabbing her slim wrists, I yanked her hands above her head. My dick was already nudging at her wet entrance.

"I see talking about serious hardware has made you wet, Mrs Barclay," I said nudging my straining head just enough to breach her entrance. Her head tilted back like she wanted me to take her then and there but I wasn't done making her wait.

"What are you waiting for? Take me?"

"Sure, darlin', where do you wanna go?" I asked still tormenting her with my dick."

"I want you inside me."

"Like this you mean?" I slid my dick deep and pulled it back to the same position. Everything in me fought not to see how amazing it had felt when her tight passage curved tightly around my cock."

Chloe wriggled, twisted, and clamped her legs around my waist, "Give it to me," she snapped. The skin on her brow creased in frustration. I leaned forward and kissed her hard my tongue demanding hers duel with mine. She promptly stopped moving and a deep muffled moan passed from her mouth to mine.

"Ah. You really want this, huh?" I asked again taking both wrists in one hand and moving the other to circle her clit. "Jesus, baby I don't need to ask if you're ready for me you're soaking down here." Chloe's eyelashes fell a little making her appear far more innocent than I knew she was. Flopping her legs from around my waist she spread them wide and arched up into me. I had no hesitation in taking her that time and I swallowed back my emotions when she allowed me to slide deep inside.

Chloe's breath hitched as her penetrative trusting stare pierced my soul. I stilled my eyes focused and only on her as we both took a little adjust to sensuality of the moment. It never ceased to amaze me how tight she was and how well we fitted together.

As soon as I'd caught my breath I pulled my ass back and slid in deeper again. A soft needy whimper left her mouth when I drove my cock to the hilt and her passive fingers became attacking claws as she scratched at the edge of my hand in a bid to break free of my hold on her wrists.

I scooted closer with my knees to give me better traction and began to fuck her harder, "Is this what you're after? You like me fucking you like this? Tell me what you want."

"Yes— like that. Do it like that," she commanded in a shaky voice as her tits bounced in mesmerizing circles while I drove it home.

"This? What else? You want me to squeeze your tits like this?" I asked letting go of her wrists and grabbing her breasts firmly as I rode her harder. Chloe's eyes rolled to the back of her head and I felt her constrict so I fucked her fast and hard.

Small contractions pulsed each tightening her muscles around my cock until her legs began to quiver. It was the exact point that always hit me square in the chest. Watching as I brought her close felt incredible.

No sooner had I seen the signs of her pending orgasm when her belly contracted hard and her legs shook uncontrollably. I clamped my hand over her mouth and her screams became muffled otherwise she'd have been heard down the hall. Not that I minded but we had Piper to think about.

Seeing Chloe lost in a wave of ecstasy was what I lived for. "Fuck, Chloe, so tight, darlin' feels incredible." When I glanced down at her tits the red grip marks I'd made on her skin looked so fucking hot and made my dick twitch deep inside her. Suddenly the familiar tightness in my stomach grew steadily and radiated down to my balls like liquid fire. A second later I shot my load in a dozen rapid pulsating spurts deep inside her.

Collapsing on top of her I held her tight and rolled back, pulling her on top again. Chloe placed her head over my chest and let out a deep contented sigh before lifting herself up again to plant a small lingering kiss over my heart. "I love you," she whispered and lay back down. A satisfied sigh of my own released for the fact even after the difficult day Chloe had faced we'd continued to keep moving forward despite the new deal we'd been served.

Normally, our sessions between the sheets would have lasted infinitely longer before I would have let myself go but the previous couple of days had been a shock for all of us and the pressure had built as a result. I'd been uncertain how Chloe would respond to my news and was thankful for how positive she behaved, but it didn't make me complacent about letting her know how much she meant to me.

Chapter Thirteen

DISTANCE

Chloe

THREE WEEKS OF ARRANGEMENTS AND GIBSON HAD MANAGED TO pull off what would have taken the rest of us a few months to achieve. A smallholding of twenty-five acres of prime land had been identified as a suitable place for Melody, her mother, and grandmother to live. Copper Mountain was a beautiful place but I figured Kiran probably hadn't wanted to be there. It was a tiny town in the middle of nowhere, but when I saw the property Gibson had chosen I changed my mind on that.

I wasn't surprised by Gibson's choice of property because he wanted his daughter to have every comfort and be well looked after. He'd been very generous especially after Kiran had kept Melody from him in the first place.

As soon as he opened the modest front door of the cabin the house took my breath away. Six thousand square feet of beautiful timber and stone lay hidden mainly from view to the rear of the property.

Two thousand square feet of living space on the floor we stood on was split into a den, a small private nook in one corner with a book-case, a second larger living room, and everything was bathed in sunlight as it shone through a huge arched window. Woodland views surrounded the back of the property with mountains to the front. I imagined Melody staring out at the lush green foliage in the summer months and the snow-covered tree tops in winter.

A massive fireplace with a natural log fire divided the middle of the room in half at one side. Plush deep cushioned couches gave the feeling of luxury and comfort while the open kitchen on the other side was probably most chef's dream.

Naturally stunning terrain surrounded a beautiful small-looking cabin from the front. Low single floor was visible and it was very unassuming at first glance. But once inside it was a fabulous space spread over three floors to the back, a huge wrap around natural pine veranda and secluded parking under the whole structure.

With five bedrooms and a large playroom one floor down I had to admit had Gibson been asked to design a house with Melody's safety in mind the cabin was as near to perfection as he'd have managed.

At first I hadn't wanted to see it, but when he explained how important it would be for me to picture what Melody was talking when she talked about where she lived. I agreed it made sense because I knew once Kiran moved in I wouldn't be running around with a pumpkin pie or anything.

I was happy that the distance between their place and ours was sufficient for me not to run into Kiran every day, yet with only five miles of travel between places I knew it would be easy for Gibson to have Melody over whenever her schedules and custody arrangements allowed.

"C'mere darlin'," I know you probably don't think I need to say this, but I'm gonna say it anyway." Outside on the decking Gibson took a deep breath and pulled me into his arms when we'd finished looking around. "Just because this is here and Melody is close doesn't mean I'm gonna be over here all the time. I'm never setting foot in here if I can help it. Emma will bring her and take her home.

"You don't have to do that, Gibson. That's not necessary. I trust you to—"

"And I trust me too, but since Kiran isn't one hundred percent all about Melody, I figured it was a safer bet not to be around her at all if I can help it. Last thing I want in all of this is her spinning a yarn in an effort to dent what we've got. Now I figure we're unshakable but fuck...I'm not giving her any ammunition. You got me?" Gibson's brow was creased from carrying the weight of his words.

Knowing there were always women who felt like he owed them a shot I accepted that his decision was as much about him as it would have been for me and smiled.

"Yes, boss, I got you." I saluted him and he caught my wrist in his hand then brought my fingers to his lips. Softly he peppered kisses on them then released his grip to slide his cold hand onto the nape of my neck, under my hair. A pleasurable shiver shot down my spine and made my panties wet instantly.

Gibson gave me his trademark roguish grin and laughed softly. "Did you come in your panties there. Your whole body shook," he rasped as he dipped his mouth to my neck.

I shoved him back and gave him a knowing smile because I hadn't missed the notable bulge he'd brushed across my tummy while his attention became more heated.

"Gibson Barclay if you think you're going to fuck me on the deck of your baby momma's house you have another think coming."

"So long as something's coming," he answered and chuckled. Instantly he bent his knees and swept my up over his shoulder with my ass in the air and my face almost level with his. "Okay, you've seen enough, I guess I need to take you home. If I'm not getting any alfresco action here I'm taking you back to the hot tub at home. How does that sound."

"Uh, no you're not. Piper is home with a tutor today," I reminded him.

"Fuck where did all these kids suddenly come from?" he asked in a tone laced with frustration. "Do I have to book into a hotel in town to fuck my wife these days?"

"There's always the pool house," I suggested because by then I was just as eager as he was.

"Good, call, Mrs. Barclay, I always knew you weren't just a pretty face...and ass," he said slapping it firmly. I yelped loudly and the noise carried. "Maybe it's time we brought another cabin on the property to use as a sneaky fuck pad. What do you think?" he asked stopping again to wait for my reply.

"Does sex dominate your thoughts all day long, Gibson?"

"What else is there to think about, darlin'?" he asked on a chuckle. "You know you love it so don't hang there pretending I don't do it for you. I'd be a terrible husband if I didn't make your toes curl and that pretty little voice of yours scream with every chance I got now, wouldn't I?"

I bit back a grin because he had a point.

"See ... I thought so," he said taking my silence as me agreeing with him. "Now let's get to that pool house. My dick is aches like fuck because it wants to be snuggled inside you." I burst out laughing because snuggle couldn't begin to describe what Gibson did to me when I let him inside me.

Arriving back at our place, Gibson was true to his word. As soon as we got out the car, he slung me unceremoniously over his shoulder and spun with me hanging upside-down to address Jonny.

"We'll be getting jiggy in the pool house, Jonny, go play with yourself." It had been a few years since I'd been embarrassed by something Gibson said but I slapped his firm ass and hurt my hand for talking like I wasn't there.

"Oh, you wanna get a little kinky, darlin'?" he suggested and jogged alongside the pool to get to the door, "Let's see...how can I make this interesting for you?" he teased as he stepped inside the living room and swung around to close the door. Placing his hand on my ass he wandered into the bedroom and ceremonially dumped me flat on my back on the bed. Our eyes met and immediately the mood in the room intensified.

"Ah. Now I've got your attention, huh? Get undressed," he commanded.

Defiance was my initially reaction and I opened my mouth to respond, but Gibson tore open the buttons on his fly and I diverted to there instead. My lips felt dry as my heartrate spiked. "Now then, look what I've got here," he said in another playful tone like he was making a craft. I softly laughed as my eyes met his until I saw his heavy semi hard cock in the palm of his hand. Gibson let out a low rumbly laugh and his hand began to tug slowly in even strokes. "You like watching this?" he asked.

I swallowed and licked my dry lips. "It's hot," I answered honestly.

"Take off your clothes, I need you naked this minute," he ordered in a low voice loaded with frustration. I grinned at his frustration and the look he gave me said a thousand words. I rose up on the bed on my knees and pulled the T-shirt I wore over my head, pulled my hair free of it and threw it on the floor.

"Now the jeans," he commanded, his hand moving steadily up and down his thick hard length. I climbed up to my feet and undid my zipper while his eyes fixed on it. Sliding them over my hips I pulled them down past my knees then dropped onto my ass on the bed and pulled them over my feet.

"You're still wearing way too much for my liking, take off the rest," he told me.

"Since when do you give all the orders around here," I asked playfully.

"Since my balls feel like baseballs hanging from the end of my dick. Do it," he snapped as his frustration grew. I smiled lovingly and lay back on the bed stretching my arms and legs wide.

"What if I said *"no"*?" I asked as I made myself comfortable.

"Really?"

"Yeah, what if I said I'm not taking my underwear off."

"Then you'll go across my knee until your ass is raw then I'll fuck you so hard you won't be able to sit down for the rest of the day for teasing me in the first place."

"Hmm. Sounds pretty aweso—" my voice died in my throat and was replaced by a yelp as Gibson dragged me swiftly down the bed, lifted me and I landed face down over his knee. A sharp crack rang out in the room and my ass cheek stung.

"Are you sorry for mocking me?"

Even though I was shocked, his sudden aggression was turning me on. "Nope," I replied laughing.

Crack, another sharp spank hit my ass and the pain that stung before hurt more. "How about now?"

It was painful but funny at the same time and I laughed harder.

"Oh, so you think this is fucking funny, do you?" he asked trying to sound mad but he couldn't fully conceal his amusement. I giggled manically because I was still lying across his knee and he started tickling me in my ribs. Breathless from laughing I tried to squirm my way off his legs.

Suddenly he held me tight, turned me around, and dropped me back on the bed. His phone clattered to the floor from the pocket of his jeans and he bent forward to pick it up. Glancing up through his lashes to meet my gaze he gave me a roguish grin and flicked through his phone.

Seconds later "I'm Gonna Do My Thing," by Royal Deluxe played from a playlist on his phone as he stepped out his jeans. Tugging free of them he crawled all the way up the bed like a predator who wasn't taking no for an answer.

Seeing how delicious and appealing he looked naked from the waist down with his tight white T- shirt stretched across his fine body the word no was no longer in my vocabulary. "Enough already. I'm topped out with all the foreplay, my dick is stretched tight to the point of pain in its skin," he snapped pretending to be angry.

Sliding his hands down over one hip he grabbed at both sides of my thong and tugged it roughly until it ripped it in half. He lifted my legs and bent them at the knee. Next he pushed them tight to my chest and hurriedly swept the bulbous thick head of his dick down my slick crease. Holding his cock in his hand he pushed forward and stretched me inch by inch as he came inside me.

As his pubic bone met mine he stilled, held his breath while we both adjusted then grunted loudly in satisfaction when he exhaled. "Damn. Best feeling in the world, darlin'," he whispered and nibbled my neck.

All of my senses were flooded by the overwhelming sensation of lying beneath the man of my dreams. The look of possessive intent was unbearable as my anticipation grew with my need for him to move inside me. "Fuck me, Gibson," I said in a stark commanding way. I saw the surprise in his eyes and the heat that followed my words.

"Oh, darlin', I fully intend on doing just that and I warned you this ain't gonna be no tender session." His forehead dropped to mine and his breath became my air as he pulled his butt back and slid back and forth for a moment. "Damn, I really wanna fuck you hard but slipping in and out of your tight wet little pussy like this feels too fucking good," he countered in an argument with himself as he rocked into me slowly. "You're a witch, you know that?" He asked in a teasing tone. "What the fuck have you done to me, Chloe Barclay?" I questioned with a cheeky grin.

"What have I done? I'm thinking it's the other way around. Anyway, you've been tantalizing me for the last two hours are you gonna fuck me or what?" I asked, challenging his previous threat to fuck me hard. No sooner had I said the words when he did just that. True to his word, Gibson definitely claimed what was his until I could no longer stand the pleasure he gave me. Exhausted and sore, but in the best way imaginable I closed my legs and curled to the side. Unable to keep my eyes open a second longer I sunk into a deep and satisfied slumber.

Chapter Fourteen

ALL RIGHT

Gibson

NORMALLY, I WASN'T OF A NERVOUS DISPOSITION. HELL, I COULDN'T walk out to a stadium of seventy thousand people without blinking if my job demanded it. Nothing usually made me feel antsy... yet waiting for my daughter to be near-by I felt exactly that.

Doubts crept in. Was I ill prepared? What if I gave her and Piper bad advice down the line? What if Melody hated me when she read about my past? What if she wouldn't listen to me when she was a teen because of how I behaved?

"I can hear you thinking," Chloe says slipping her arms around me from behind and placing her cheek between my shoulder blades. Her touch instantly grounded me. I turned in her arms and faced her. My hands slipped to her lower back and I clasped my fingers together and looked down at her concerned expression.

"You're all that, you know that?"

"No you are," she replied.

"Aren't I entitled to my opinion?"

"I suppose...everything's gonna be all right, you know that?" Chloe's reassurance was well-timed.

I inhaled deeply and thought it had to be no matter what. "I know."

"Then stop worrying. If anyone should be uneasy about this it should be me."

"I know. Thank you... for trusting me...for accepting Melody."

Instead of replying Chloe reached up on tiptoe and brushed my dry lips with hers.

"Then let's get ready, she'll be here in twenty minutes."

Stepping backward out of my embrace she took my hand. "Just be you, Gibson. She may be a child but you have this innate ability to draw people toward you. She'll adore you...like you already adore her."

"Maybe I should hire you as my life coach."

Chloe bit her lip before they twisted into a sassy expression. She raked her eyes over me. "Sorry Mr Barclay, you couldn't afford my rates." Swiftly I patted her ass and scooped her into my side.

"Smart ass," I shot back and glanced toward the house. Together we walked in silence both knowing from that day forward our time alone would be governed by Melody and Piper's schedules and our own needs would have to take a different path for us to achieve a balance.

We knew whatever happened and however we chose to bring up our girls their lives wouldn't be conventional. They'd already led lives outside the norm at the point when we met them, but we'd parent them with love. Even if sometimes that love was 'tough love' to keep them from making life-changing mistakes.

Between Chloe and I we had a wealth of knowledge of the bad decisions and experiences we'd endured during our own journeys and I figured that *had* to count when helping to guide kids of our own.

The grinding of gravel alerted us as to Melody's arrival and Chloe slid her hands around my waist on the other side of the door. "I know you're going to be an amazing dad, Gibson. Take a breath, take it slow, and enjoy her."

My throat closed with emotion for the humility Chloe had to ensure I felt at ease when her heart must have been aching for the child that we lost. "Melody may have a birth mom, Chloe, but I'm gonna make sure you're given the same respect and honor the title of Mom brings with it."

"No, Gibson it's not up to you to force the issue. It's up to me to earn it."

Before I could reply the door burst open and Melody stood breathless, her little chest heaving excitedly and her wide almond shaped eyes searching and bright. "I'm here, Daddy," she screeched before running full pelt and lunging at me with a pink, Little Mermaid backpack jiggling behind her.

Bending my knees I caught her flicking her legs up in the air and hung her upside down by her ankles. Squealing with delight she shouted, "Chloe tell him to put me down, help me," she said, giggling. I turned her right side up and planted her firmly on her feet where she staggered off balance and latched on to Chloe's leg.

Grinning she looked up at Chloe and shook her head, "Jeez, how do you deal with that, my daddy's a real handful, huh?" she asked wiping her bangs out of her eyes and smiling at Chloe like she'd known her for years.

"You're right Melody, he can be a handful at times, but I'm glad he's *my* handful," she answered honestly.

"Well, just as well I'm coming to live here sometimes. I'll try and give you a break." Chloe and I both chuckled at her grown-up attitude as she clung tighter to my wife's leg.

I don't know why but I felt Melody was looking for acceptance from Chloe just as much as Chloe needed Melody to like her. "I heard my mom talking on the phone and she said my daddy could have any woman in the world but he picked you. That means you're very special, right?"

Biting back a grin I could well imagine that conversation but I was glad what Melody took from it.

"You're right, baby girl, she's the most special lady in the world to me and you and Piper are the two most special girls."

Melody squeezed Chloe's leg tighter and waved me in for a group hug. "I'm so glad my mommy found you Daddy because I know I'm going to have so much fun here with all of you. And I'm going to be a rock star just like you."

Lifting Melody into my arms I pulled Chloe close and kissed the top of her head. "Yeah? Over my dead body you are." I answered in an amused tone, but as I looked into Melody's eyes I felt my heart melt once again and figured putting my foot down like I promised myself was suddenly not going to be as easy in practice as I'd imagined.

The End
Want to know more about Piper?
Look out for Follow the Music: Piper's story
in the next Last Score series novella.
Don't want to miss it? Sign up to my newsletter today.

NEWSLETTER: http://bit.ly/KLShandwicknewsletter

Gibson's Melody is a Last Score novella if you'd like to read the full story of Gibson and Chloe check out Gibson's Legacy book1 and Trusting Gibson book 2 (Last Score) series here.
My Book
My Book

ABOUT THE AUTHOR

K. L. Shandwick lives on the outskirts of London. She started writing after a challenge by a friend when she commented on a book she read. The result of this was "The Everything Trilogy." Her background has been mainly in the health and social care sector in the U.K. She is still currently a freelance or self- employed professional in this field. Her books tend to focus on the relationships of the main characters. Writing is a form of escapism for her and she is just as excited to find out where her characters take her as she is when she reads another author's work.

Pinterest:
https://uk.pinterest.com/kshandwick/
Newsletter:
http://eepurl.com/bik4Qr
BOOKBUB:
https://www.bookbub.com/authors/k-l-shandwick
AMAZON PAGE:
author.to/klshandwick
ALLAUTHOR:
http://klshandwick.allauthor.com/
TUMBLR:
https://www.tumblr.com/search/klshandwick
INSTAGRAM:
https://www.instagram.com/klshandwick
GOODREADS:
https://www.goodreads.com/author/show/7581125.K_L_Shandwick

K.L. SHANDWICK'S HANGOUT:
http://bit.ly/klshandwickhangout

For more information...
www.klshandwick.com/

OTHER BOOKS BY K.L. SHANDWICK

Enough Isn't Everything

http://bit.ly/EnoughIsntEverythingUS

http://bit.ly/EnoughIsntEverythingUK

http://bit.ly/EnoughIsntEverythingAmazonCA

http://bit.ly/EnoughIsntEverythingAmazonAU

Everything She Needs

http://bit.ly/EverythingSheNeedsUS

http://bit.ly/EverythingSheNeedsUK

http://bit.ly/EverythingSheNeedsCA

http://bit.ly/EverythingSheNeedsAU

Everything I Want

http://bit.ly/EverythingIWantUS

http://bit.ly/EverythingIWantUK

http://bit.ly/EverythingIWantCA

http://bit.ly/EverythingIWantAU

Ready For Flynn, Part1

http://bit.ly/ReadyForFlynnPart1US

http://bit.ly/ReadyForFlynnPart1UK

http://bit.ly/ReadyForFlynnPart1AU

http://bit.ly/ReadyForFlynnPart1CA

Ready For Flynn, Part2

http://bit.ly/ReadyForFlynnPart2US

http://bit.ly/ReadyForFlynnPart2UK

http://bit.ly/ReadyForFlynnPart2AU

http://bit.ly/ReadyForFlynnPart2CA

Ready For Flynn, Part3

http://bit.ly/ReadyForFlynnPart3US

http://bit.ly/ReadyForFlynnPart3UK

http://bit.ly/ReadyForFlynnPart3AU

http://bit.ly/ReadyForFlynnPart3CA

Notes On Love

http://bit.ly/NotesOnLoveUS

http://bit.ly/NotesOnLoveUK

http://bit.ly/NotesOnLoveAU

http://bit.ly/UNotesOnLoveCA

Missing Beats

https://www.books2read.com/u/bMGzE5

27410120R00070

Printed in Great Britain
by Amazon